"Explore on your own!" Dirk thundered

He shook his head in disgust. "You stupid tourists make me sick! Didn't anyone warn you that there are grizzly bears out there? Do you have any idea what a grizzly could do to a face like yours with one sweep of its paw?"

"Well, I'm sorry!" Nicole cried. "But I'm getting a little sick of being yelled at. I'm grateful to you for rescuing me. My father will reward you handsomely for your trouble, I assure you. Now, if you'll just take me back to the hotel and—"

"Try to get this through your head," he snarled. "It's too late. There's no way we could get fifty feet in this blizzard, much less the five miles back to Many Glaciers Hotel. I'm stuck with you."

Rosemary Hammond lives on the West Coast, but has traveled extensively with her husband throughout the United States, Mexico and Canada. She loves to write and has been fascinated by the mechanics of fiction ever since her college days. She reads extensively, enjoying everything from Victorian novels to mysteries, spy stories and, of course, romances.

Books by Rosemary Hammond

TWO DIFFERENT WORLDS

Rosemary Hammond

Harlequin Books

TORONTO • NEW YORK • LONDON
AMSTERDAM • PARIS • SYDNEY • HAMBURG
STOCKHOLM • ATHENS • TOKYO • MILAN

Original hardcover edition published in 1990
by Mills & Boon Limited

ISBN 0-373-03165-3

Harlequin Romance first edition December 1991

TWO DIFFERENT WORLDS

CHAPTER ONE

NICOLE glowered down at the ground and plodded onward. For the sake of privacy, she and her father dropped some distance behind the small group that was following the guide up the steep rocky path, and by now she was so angry that she didn't trust herself even to speak to him.

She was also tired and cold and hungry. Although a pale sun was shining directly overhead, the curving path had brought them into the shadow of yet another snow-covered mountain peak, and to the north lay a solid mass of dark clouds.

'A glacier is like a huge river of ice,' the guide was explaining. 'The largest one in the park covers about three square miles and moves downhill at the rate of a few inches a day. Here in northern Montana...'

Nicole wasn't listening. She just wanted to leave, to go back to California and the comforts of her own home in Beverly Hills. Why her father had insisted on dragging her here to this godforsaken place to spring his brilliant scheme on her was more than she could understand.

'Nicole,' he said to her now in a low voice. 'Nicole, you're just being stubborn. Victor's a fine man. All I'm asking you to do is consider his proposal.'

She raised her head and turned to him, dark eyes blazing. 'I already told Victor a hundred times I wouldn't marry him. Why are you putting pressure on me now?'

'I already explained that. The company is over-extended. I need Victor's capital to get on my feet again.'

'You want to *sell* me!' she bit out. 'Is that it?'

His jaw hardened. 'Of course not. I only want what's best for you.'

'Marrying Victor Channing is *not* what's best for me!'

'Nicole,' he said with a sigh, 'you're twenty-five years old. It's about time you settled down, and I have yet to see the man who could please you. There's nothing wrong with Victor, and you have to marry someone.'

'If you're saying you don't want to support me any longer,' she said stiffly, 'then I'll go out and get a job of my own.'

'That's not fair. I've never made you do one thing you didn't want to do, never denied your slightest wish. Why won't you just think about it before turning him down? That's all I ask.'

Nicole came to a sudden halt and faced her father directly. 'Because my mind is already made up,' she said flatly. 'I don't love Victor Channing. I never have. I never will.'

Stamping her foot in sheer frustration, she turned abruptly off the main path on to a smaller one that wound upward through the trees. As she stalked off, her hands in the pockets of her heavy jacket, her head down against the chill wind, she heard the guide call to her.

'Miss West—please stay on the main path!'

'I'll be right back,' she called over her shoulder. 'I just want to take a closer look at the wild flowers up on that knoll.'

'Well, don't go far,' he replied dubiously. 'We really should all stay together.'

Unheeding, spurred on by her anger, Nicole plunged ahead blindly, desperate to be alone for a while so that she could sort things out in her mind. From time to time she could hear faint voices calling to her from a distance, but she kept on climbing upward, scrambling over rocks and avoiding fallen branches.

It didn't really begin to occur to her that she might be lost until the wind suddenly picked up and the heavy bank of clouds that had been hovering far to the north that morning moved in directly overhead, blocking out the pale sun and filling the whole sky with an ominous dark grey canopy.

When it started to snow, at first just a light pattering of tiny flakes, she stopped short and looked around uncertainly at the unfamiliar terrain. Perhaps it was time to retrace her steps and rejoin the others.

But where was the path? The snow, which was now coming down in earnest, had covered the narrow dirt footpath completely in just the few moments it had taken her to make up her mind to go back. With its white blanket of snow, the vast steep slope that fell away before her was totally unfamiliar, and each towering evergreen looked exactly the same as all the others.

How far had she come by herself? She hadn't been gone that long—half an hour at the most. A city girl born and bred, she had no conception of distances up here in this wild mountainous country.

With a growing sense of dismay, she started to run, she hoped back down the way she had come, slipping and sliding on the fast-freezing snow, certain that she would see the hotel just over the next rise or around the next curve. By now a veritable blizzard swirled around her, and she could barely see her hand in front of her face, much less a familiar landmark.

At the top of a small knoll, she stopped and started to call for help. She stood there and shouted until she was hoarse, but the driving snow only muffled her cries, and, if there was any answer, she couldn't hear it.

I'm going to die! she thought in a sudden panic. I'm going to wander around until I drop, then just lie down and freeze to death. Half crazed by now with cold and fear, she merely followed blind instinct. Keep moving! She had to keep moving!

Finally, after what seemed like hours of going around in circles, sobbing and gasping, her teeth chattering with cold and fear, she saw just around the next bend a wreath of smoke rising up into the snow-laden sky.

With a loud cry, she plunged forward. Immediately her foot came up against a large hard object, invisible under its white covering. A sharp, searing pain jabbed up her right leg, and, just before losing consciousness, she felt herself falling, falling...

When she came to, the first sensation that gripped her was the agonising pain in her leg, the second that she was being carried, jostled along unceremoniously, each jolt sending a new shaft of fire through her injured leg.

She opened her eyes and looked up to see, looming above her, a grim face framed in a fur hood. He was obviously a man; his heavy black beard was dotted with snowflakes, his eyes narrowed into slits, an angry determined set to his hard jaw. Nicole stiffened in his arms. Had she escaped being frozen to death only to be carried off by some wild mountain caveman, perhaps to be raped and murdered?

Uncaring of the pain in her leg, she began to struggle, but with a muttered curse he only tightened his grip on her and continued on without a word. No match for his superior physical strength, she closed her eyes and silently tried to prepare herself for the worst.

After a while he slowed his pace, and when Nicole cautiously opened her eyes again they were approaching a rough wooden cabin. The smoke coming out of the brick chimney told her that it must be what she'd seen before she fainted.

The man kicked the door open and stepped inside into a blessed warmth. He nudged the door shut with his shoulder, then stalked across the room and set her down on her feet. She cried out, her injured leg buckling under her weight, and started to fall. He reached out for her before she hit the floor and guided her, limping, to a chair.

When the pain had diminished, she looked up at him warily. What she saw did nothing to reassure her. He had pushed the hood back from his face to reveal a thick head of tousled black hair that covered his ears and the back of his neck. The snow had melted from his beard, and it was as thick and black as the hair on his head.

He stood silently before her, his long legs apart, his knuckles resting on his hips, glaring down at her as though she were some particularly loathsome form of insect.

'Just what the hell do you think you're doing out here alone?' he bit out angrily.

'I—I guess I got lost,' she said in a small voice. 'I couldn't find the path, and then I hurt my leg and——'

'Don't you know that the Forest Service regulations explicitly state that no one—without exception—is ever to go anywhere in Glacier Park without a guide?'

'Well, yes,' she stammered. 'And we did have a guide. I just wanted to explore a little on my own, and then——'

'Explore on your own!' he thundered. He shook his head in disgust. 'Lord, you tourists make me sick! Didn't anyone warn you that there are grizzly bears out there just waiting for stupid little girls like you to disturb them? Do you have any idea what a grizzly can do to a face like yours with one swipe of its paw?'

'Well, I'm sorry!' she cried. 'Can't you let me finish just one sentence? I'm getting a little sick of being yelled at. I'm grateful to you for rescuing me. My father will reward you handsomely for your trouble, I can assure you. Now, if you'll just take me back to the hotel, my leg needs looking after and——'

'Damn it!' he shouted. 'I *can't* take you back!'

His face was livid, his eyes burning with fury, and as he took a step towards her, one hand raised menacingly in the air, she cowered back from him in the chair and gazed at him wide-eyed.

'What do you mean?' she whispered.

He dropped the hand to his side and glared down at her. 'Try to get this through your head,' he snarled. 'It's too late. There's no way we could get fifty feet in this blizzard, much less the five miles back to Many Glacier Hotel. I'm stuck with you.'

If he had hit her, which he was obviously longing to do, the hostility in his tone couldn't have been more clear. If what he said was true, then she was trapped here with this wild man for heaven knew how long.

But was he telling the truth? Why should she believe him? He could be a kidnapper who knew they were staying at the hotel, knew of her famous father's wealth and prestige. He'd hold her for ransom, then kill her. She had to get out of there, somehow make her way back to civilisation.

She rose unsteadily to her feet, testing her weight on the injured leg. It didn't seem quite so bad now. Eyeing him warily, she began to inch her way towards the door, hanging on to furniture for support. As she passed by him, she expected him to reach out and grab her, but instead he merely folded his arms across his chest and watched her, a mocking smile curling his thin mouth.

'And just where do you think you're going?' he enquired nastily.

'I'm leaving,' she announced in her loftiest tone. 'And don't try to stop me.'

He dipped his dark head and made a sweeping gesture with one hand. 'I wouldn't dream of it,' he said. 'Please. Be my guest.'

She had reached the door by now, and when she opened it she was almost knocked over by a sharp gust of wind, the driving snow stinging her eyes and face. She slammed the door shut and turned around to face him, leaning weakly back against it.

For a long moment they simply stood there staring at each other. There was utter silence in the room, with only the crackling of the fire in the stone hearth and the wind outside to break the stillness. Finally, Nicole's shoulders sagged and she slowly made her way back to the chair. It was hopeless. She was a prisoner here. There was no way out.

Then the tears of self-pity welled up behind her eyes. Was she really doomed? She looked at him out of the corner of her eye. He had turned away from her, and she watched as he shed his heavy fur-lined jacket, revealing worn jeans and a red plaid woollen shirt. Then, ignoring her completely, he sat down on a chair and began to take off his boots.

'What are you doing?' she asked.

'What does it look like I'm doing?' he retorted. 'I'm taking off my boots.'

Nicole glanced around the cabin. It was built of rough-hewn cedar logs with patches of white plaster filling in the chinks. A fire was blazing in a stone fireplace. At one end was a window, and beneath it a counter covered with cans of food and what looked like a hotplate. There was a table at that end made of unfinished wood, a hurricane lamp set on top of it.

At the other end of the room was a narrow bed, neatly made and covered with a bright Indian blanket. Next to it sat a desk, piled high with books and papers. A map hung on the wall above it. The two of them were sitting on the only chairs, but there was a shabby couch set directly in front of the fireplace.

It certainly didn't look like the hideaway of a kidnapper or a mad rapist. Nicole glanced back at the man. He had risen from the chair and was standing at the counter by the window, bent over, lighting the hotplate, which was apparently fuelled by some kind of gas. Of course, there would be no electricity. He was ignoring her presence entirely; she wasn't used to that.

With a lift of her chin, she called out to him in her most imperious tone, 'If as you say we're trapped, may I ask what you're doing here?'

Without a word he continued puttering with the stove for several moments, until he had it adjusted to his satisfaction. Then he turned slowly around and leaned back against the counter.

'I have work to do here,' he gritted through his teeth. 'And the last thing I need is to have someone like you on my hands.'

'What kind of work could you possibly have up here? This is a national park, intended for tourists.'

'It's also an important wildlife preserve, funded by both the Federal Government and the State of Montana. I'm a wildlife biologist, here to study the winter migration and hibernation patterns of the indigenous species.'

'You mean like bears and wolves?' she asked, alarmed.

He nodded. 'Among others.'

She rose to her feet and limped towards him. 'Listen,' she said, 'I don't want to be here any more than you want me here. You must have some way of communicating with the outside world.'

He nodded again. 'There's a radio.'

Suddenly filled with new hope, she flashed him a bright smile. 'Well then, all you have to do is call the hotel,' she said eagerly. 'My father is probably frantic with worry by now. I can promise he'll reward you handsomely if you can get me back safely.'

'Believe me,' he replied fervently, 'reward or no reward, there's nothing that would please me more. But, as it happens, the damned radio just conked out on me this morning.'

Nicole widened her eyes in horror. 'But that can't be!' she cried. 'I mean, what will you do? How will you survive?'

He shrugged. 'I have enough provisions here to last me for several weeks. The Forest Service boys know I'm here. When they find they can't raise me on the radio, they'll come to make sure I'm OK.'

'Oh, well then,' she said with relief, 'that's all right. When do you expect them?'

He laughed sharply. 'Not until this blizzard is over, and probably not for some time after that. It's September, the end of the tourist season. They have enough to do getting ready for winter.' He eyed her narrowly and crossed over to her side. 'What are you doing here at Glacier so late in the season, anyway?'

'My father wanted to come,' she replied simply.

He raised one heavy dark eyebrow. 'And do you always obey your father?' he asked in a sardonic mocking tone.

She flushed deeply. 'As a matter of fact, no,' she replied in a curt voice. 'Not about important things.'

He stared at her for several seconds, then said, 'What's your name?'

'Nicole—Nicole West. My father is——'

He made an impatient gesture with his hand, cutting her off. 'I don't care who your father is. He could be the President of the United States, and he still couldn't get you out of here.'

He turned from her and strode back over to the counter, where the pan of water he had set on the stove was beginning to boil. She sank back down on the hard chair and watched him as he leaned over to turn down the burner. Then he straightened up, reached into the cupboard and took down two tin mugs.

All his movements were graceful and controlled, with no wasted or clumsy motion. There was an air of certainty about him, as though he always knew exactly what he was doing and planned every step carefully before he acted. Just like her father!

He looked to be quite a strong man too, the chest and shoulders broad under the heavy shirt, the hips narrow in the worn jeans. He would be quite attractive, Nicole thought, if it weren't for the heavy beard and the thick rumpled hair that curled down over his neck clear to his shirt collar. And the nasty disposition.

As she watched, she pondered her situation with a sinking heart. Was she really stuck out here with this man? And for how long? From the day she was born, she'd had her father's wealth at her disposal, protecting her from all the unpleasantness of life, with servants to do her bidding, money available for every whim, all her material desires provided for.

Now here she was, without a stitch of clothing except what she had on her back, no make-up, no shops, no hairdresser to tend her elaborate coiffure, not even any money.

Exhausted from her ordeal on the mountainside, her sore leg still throbbing, she felt her eyes grow heavy, her head nodding, and then only blankness.

When she came to, she was lying on top of the narrow bed. Her jacket and boots had been removed, and she was loosely covered with the bright Indian blanket. She raised her head and looked around groggily. With a sharp, swift jab of dismay it came back to her where she was and how she had got there. She was trapped, on this mountain, in this cabin, and with this man.

He was sitting at the desk, just beyond the foot of the bed, his elbow propped up, his shaggy head resting on his fist, apparently deeply engrossed in what looked to be a large book of maps or charts. Occasionally he would frown, flip the pages, then hurriedly scribble in the open notebook beside him.

There was a distinct aroma of food in the air, and, in spite of her anxiety over the awful predicament she was in, the lingering fear of this silent, menacing man, Nicole's stomach began to churn with hunger. She'd had nothing to eat since breakfast, hours ago, and even then she'd been so angry at her father that she'd only picked at a piece of toast.

As though sensing that she was watching him, the man turned his head abruptly and stared at her through half-closed eyes. She quailed inwardly under that steady, wordless gaze, and when he suddenly shoved his chair back and rose to his feet she drew the blanket up to her chin and cowered back defensively against the hard pillow.

Instead of leaping over to attack her, however, he merely spread his arms and stretched widely, flexing his back muscles, clenching and unclenching his cramped fingers. Then he turned away and ambled over to the stove, where he began to stir something in a pot sitting there.

Still eyeing him warily, Nicole slowly rose up to a sitting position. He didn't seem to mean her any harm, at least not for the moment, and her mouth was watering at the mere thought of food.

'I'm very hungry,' she said stiffly. 'Could I please have something to eat?'

'Sure,' he replied. Without turning around, he kept on with his stirring.

'Thank you,' she said, and waited while he ladled out whatever was in the pan into a dish.

At this point she wasn't fussy about what she ate, so long as it was food, and as he came towards her, the steam still rising from the plate, she smiled pleasantly at him and reached out for it.

Without even glancing her way, he made straight for his desk, sat down and started shovelling in the food. Nicole's mouth fell open. All she could do was stare at him. Apparently, as far as he was concerned, she might as well not even exist!

'Don't I get any?' she spluttered at last.

He glanced over at her. 'I already said you could,' he replied, elaborate patience in every syllable. He waved his fork in the direction of the stove. 'Help yourself.'

'But what about my leg? Surely you don't expect me to walk on it?'

'Have you tried?'

'Well, no, but——'

'Then you'd better start,' he broke in. The tone of finality in his voice was unmistakable.

'It could be broken,' she protested loudly.

'I doubt it,' he replied in a dry tone.

Nicole opened her mouth to argue, but when he swivelled around in his chair to glower over at her, she snapped it shut tight.

'Listen,' he said flatly, 'it's bad enough that I'm stuck with you here at all. If you think I'm going to wait on you besides, you're out of your mind.'

Nicole was seized with the sudden certain conviction that he would actually let her starve before he'd serve her one morsel of food. That was, if he didn't turn her out in the snow altogether. It would serve him right if she did starve to death. How would he explain that to her father?

Immediately she realised the stupidity of that idea. Talk about cutting off your nose to spite your face! Gingerly she swung her legs over the side of the bed. Supporting herself with one hand braced against the wall, she stood up on her good left leg. Gradually she lowered her right leg to the floor, testing her weight on it.

It still hurt, but he was probably right, it wasn't actually broken, and she soon found that by dragging it behind her and hanging on to furniture as she went she actually could make it over to the counter. Conscious of his silent appraisal every step of the way, she was torn between showing him how capable she really was, how little she needed his help, and limping a little more than she really needed to just to make him feel ashamed of himself for the shabby way he was treating her.

In the end, she opted for self-sufficiency and did her best to walk as straight and tall as possible. It would be a hopeless task to arouse a feeling of guilt or pity in that hard heart. The man didn't seem to have an ounce of humanity in him.

When she finally arrived at the stove and gazed down into the pan, she wrinkled her nose in distaste when she saw the soggy mass of what looked like beans and half-cooked fatty bacon lying inside. Still, it smelled good. She reached up into the cupboard, took down a metal plate, spooned in some of the beans and ate them hungrily where she stood.

It wasn't a gourmet dish by any means, but as it went down it seemed like the best meal she'd ever had in her life. It was amazing what real hunger could do, a state she had never experienced before in her life, and when she was through she felt as though she just might live.

Sighing with satisfaction, she limped her way over to the couch and sat down in front of the fire, where she wasn't facing the man directly, but could see him out of the corner of her eye. He was still deeply absorbed in his work, and as she watched him she began to wonder about him.

'Do you have a name?' she asked in a light tone.

'Morgan,' he muttered under his breath, without even raising his eyes. 'Dirk Morgan.'

'Well, Mr Morgan,' she said brightly, 'since we're obviously going to be stuck here together——'

His head swivelled around. 'It's *Dr* Morgan,' he snarled. 'I told you—I'm a biologist.' He turned back to his work.

Nicole jumped to her feet, uncaring of the swift shaft of pain that shot up her leg. With her fists clenched at her sides, her face blazing with fury, she began to shout at him.

'Well,' she cried, '*Dr* Morgan! I'd appreciate it if just once you'd let me finish a sentence.' She took a step towards the desk. 'I don't like this situation any better than you do,' she went on in a shaky voice. 'Less, I'm sure. But I'm a human being, *Dr* Morgan, and it wouldn't hurt you to treat me like one.'

Slowly he rose to his feet and turned around to face her, his eyes sweeping her up and down in an insolent appraisal. His mouth curled in a mocking, mirthless grin, and he began walking slowly towards her, menace in every step he took.

Nicole put a hand to her throat. Now I've done it, she thought. He's coming in for the kill. As he came closer, she drew back a step, raised her chin and stood her ground.

'Just stop right there,' she said loudly and firmly. 'If you harm me in any way, I can promise you that my father will see to it that you spend the rest of your life behind bars!'

He stopped inches away from her and stood stock-still, his arms crossed over his chest, a disgusted look on his face.

'Listen, lady,' he said, his voice dripping with contempt, 'I've never had to force myself on a woman yet, and I'm not about to start with a spoilt brat like you.'

Nicole ran a hand nervously through her hair, which by now was a tangled mass. Something in his voice, his very stance, the look in his eye, told her that he was telling the truth. She really didn't have anything to fear from him. In fact, he had made it quite clear that she didn't even appeal to him on *that* level.

'What's more,' he continued, 'you'd better get it through your head right now that I'm not your servant, not now, not ever. I have important work to do. I may be stuck with you, but, believe me, while you're here you're damn well going to pull your own weight. You can start by washing up the dishes.'

Nicole had never washed a dish in her life, and for a moment she was tempted to tell him the dirty dishes could pile up until doomsday before she'd touch one of them. But then she had to admit he did have a point. She looked at him. He hadn't budged.

'All right,' she said with a toss of her head, 'I will.'

She limped ostentatiously over to the desk, picked up his plate, then dragged herself across the room, muttering to herself as she went, and aware of his watchful eyes upon her every step of the way. When she reached the cooking area, she looked around helplessly. There was no sink, no hot water tap. She hadn't the faintest notion of how to begin.

She stood there for several moments debating. Finally she turned to face him. 'Where's the hot water?' she asked stiffly.

With an elaborate sigh, he got up and strode across the room towards her. She moved quickly aside as he grabbed the bucket that was sitting at one end of the counter. Then he carried it over to the door, opening it just wide enough to get the pail through.

In a few seconds, he slammed the door shut against the wind and came back with the bucket full of snow. He took the empty pot off the burner, set the pail on it and turned to her.

'That's how you get hot water around here,' he announced.

Nicole gazed up at him. His dark hair was sprinkled with white flakes, and she fought down a sudden impulse to reach up and brush them off. For one brief moment their eyes met, and for the first time she noticed that his were an odd shade of emerald-green, with dark golden flecks. He also had long coal-black lashes that any woman would envy.

'Thank you,' she muttered, and quickly turned away.

By the time she finished washing up the few dishes, she was dead tired. The short nap she'd had that afternoon hadn't begun to restore either her spirits or her energy, and as she put the last plate away in the cupboard she began to wonder apprehensively about the sleeping arrangements.

On the basis that the direct approach had to be better than waiting around for any of *his* orders, she limped over to the bed, lifted up the Indian blanket and started to shake it out. As the clouds of dust flew off it, Dirk Morgan lifted his head from his work and gave her a dirty look.

'What the hell do you think you're doing?' he barked.

'I'm getting ready to go to bed. This blanket is filthy.'

He rose to his feet and pointed at the lumpy couch. 'That's where you sleep,' he announced in a tone of utter finality.

'I can't sleep there!' she cried.

'Well, somebody has to,' he shot back at her. 'And it's not going to be me.' He grinned maliciously. 'Unless you intend to share the bed.' He glanced down at it. 'It's a little narrow, but we could probably manage. You look to be pretty skinny under all those clothes, and I'm a very heavy sleeper.'

Nicole shot him a look of such malevolence that a normal man would have quailed before it, but his mocking smile didn't waver. With a silent curse she snatched up the blanket and went over to the couch. Before settling herself, she glanced at him again. He was still standing there, his hands on his hips, watching her.

'I assume you have extra blankets,' she said loftily. 'Or did you plan on cutting it in half so we could share that too?'

To her amazement, he threw back his head and laughed, this time with genuine amusement. When he looked at her again, his mouth still twitching, his face was transformed. The hard lines were gone, and, although the beard and long hair still gave him a forbidding air, Nicole had her first glimpse of the human being that lay beneath the rough exterior.

'No,' he said at last, 'we won't have to resort to that. There are plenty of blankets. You go ahead and get some sleep. If the storm has passed over by tomorrow, we just might be able to get you out of here in one piece.'

'What do you mean?' she asked quickly. 'Are we in any danger from your wild animals?'

'Not at all,' he replied with a shrug. Then he grinned again. 'I meant before I killed you from sheer annoyance.' He shook his head. 'You're an exasperating woman, Nicole West. Now, get to bed and don't bother me any more. I have work to do.'

Too tired to think of a clever retort, Nicole settled herself on the lumpy couch with as much dignity as she could muster and covered herself with the blanket. It was warm in front of the fire and, instead of agonising over her predicament, as she'd expected, she fell almost immediately into a sound sleep.

CHAPTER TWO

THE next morning Nicole awoke to the smell of coffee and the sudden sickening realisation of where she was and what had happened the day before. Her injured leg throbbed painfully, every muscle in her body was cramped and sore from sleeping on the lumpy couch, and she felt as though she hadn't had a bath or change of clothes for at least a month.

As she blinked her eyes open, she could see that a faint light shone palely through the uncurtained window over the cooking area. Although it was still snowing, it wasn't coming down quite as heavily as it had the day before, and her spirits rose considerably. With any luck, she might be able to leave today.

Dirk Morgan was standing at the cook stove, his back to her, laying strips of bacon in a frying pan. Apparently hearing her stir, he turned around, and she braced herself for another outbreak of hostilities. Instead, when he spoke, his tone was much softer than before, actually almost pleasant.

'The storm seems to be passing,' he said cheerfully.

'That's good,' she said.

'Although you never know about these mountain blizzards,' he went on. 'There are still some dark clouds up north. However, let's think positive thoughts and assume the worst is over.'

Groaning silently, Nicole raised herself up and stretched her cramped legs out in front of her. She had slept badly, not only because of her leg, but because the lumpy couch was so uncomfortable. It had several loose springs, and no matter which way she had shifted her position during the night one of them always seemed to be jabbing her.

'The bathroom facilities aren't exactly Hilton quality,' Dirk went on, 'and you'll have to take a short trip out the back through the snow to get there, but it's clean, and I've heated you some water to wash in.'

'Thanks,' she said, rising to her feet and sniffing the air. The bacon was now sizzling in the pan and it smelled wonderful.

'Breakfast will be ready in fifteen minutes,' he called to her. 'That give you enough time to clean up?'

'Yes.' She glanced down at her wrinkled blouse and ski pants. 'Although there's not an awful lot I can do, with no clothes except what I've got on.' She crossed over to him and lifted the steaming pan of water off the stove.

'Can you manage that all right?' he asked.

Nicole gave him a suspicious look. 'You seem to be in a better mood this morning,' she commented drily.

He shrugged. 'As I said, it looks as though it could quit snowing any time now.'

Of course, she thought. With the storm letting up, he was looking forward to getting rid of her. No wonder he was feeling so chipper! In fact, as he went back to his cooking, he actually started to hum a little under his breath.

In the morning light he didn't look nearly so rough or dangerous as he had yesterday. He seemed clean, at least, and while the beard was still in place it looked as though he had shaved around it. Although he obviously wasn't the kind of man to bother with any such niceties as cologne or after-shave, there was a fresh scent of soap about him that she found somehow reassuring, even quite pleasant.

He was turning the bacon in the pan. 'With any luck we should be able to get you out of here today. The radio is still on the blink, but since your father is such an important man I'm sure he'll have a heli-copter out searching for you before long.'

By the time Nicole had trudged out through the snow to the crude bathroom facilities and finished her meagre ablutions, however, she saw to her dismay that the wind seemed to have picked up again, and she had to fight her way the ten yards back to the cabin in what looked to be the fore-runner of another howling blizzard.

Struggling against the wind, her head down, the snow filling her boots and seeping down the back of her neck, she finally made it to the door. Flinging it open, she threw herself inside and slammed it behind her, then leaned back against it, still panting from exertion.

'It's storming again out there,' she said accusingly.

Dirk was sitting at the wooden table, calmly eating his breakfast, a forkful of bacon and eggs halfway to his mouth, and poring over the open notebook that lay beside his plate. At her words, he put a finger on the book to mark his place and raised an eyebrow at her.

'I noticed,' he said curtly.

He shoved the food in his mouth, started chewing and turned back to his book, dismissing her as though she weren't even there.

Nicole was not used to being ignored. She stood there glaring at him, anger rising within her like a hot flame. Finally, literally speechless with frustration, she stalked across the room to the table and stood over him, breathing hard, her fists clenching and unclenching at her sides.

'Well?' she cried dramatically at last. 'Are you just going to sit there feeding your face?'

He sighed with elaborate patience, put a finger on his place again, and his eyes flicked up at her in a brief glance of annoyance.

'What do you expect me to do about it?' he asked. 'Shall I go out and threaten the storm? Shake my fist at it and tell it to stop? Or perhaps plead with it? Maybe if we told it what an important man your father is, it would stop out of sheer terror.'

Nicole gave him a withering look. 'There's no need to be sarcastic. I'd just like to know how in the world I'm going to get out of here.'

'You're not,' he stated flatly. 'At least not until this new storm blows over.' He gestured with his fork at the plate across the table from him. 'You'd better eat your eggs before they get cold.'

'I'm not hungry,' she muttered sulkily.

She flounced over to the blazing fire and sank down on the lumpy couch. One of the loose springs that had kept her awake half the night pinged under her weight and jabbed her sharply in the bottom.

She jumped up with a cry of exasperation and glared down at the couch.

When she heard his low chuckle behind her, she whirled around, her mouth open to deliver another stinging accusation, but when she saw the look of genuine amusement that lit up his stern features the words died on her lips. It *did* have its humorous side, after all.

Not for worlds, however, would she admit that to him. She gave him a cold haughty look, and, gathering all her dignity, walked slowly and sedately over to the table. She sat down and started to eat. Even though the eggs were stone-cold by now, they tasted delicious, and when she had finished she felt as though she just might live through this ordeal.

Dirk got up and poured himself a fresh cup of coffee, then sat back down and lit a cigarette, blowing out smoke contentedly, his eyes still glued to his notebook. As the smoke drifted across the table towards her, Nicole frowned and waved it away.

'I'd really rather you didn't smoke,' she said stiffly.

'That's too bad,' he said, and took another deep drag.

'Well?' she demanded angrily. 'Is that all you have to say?'

He gave her a weary look. 'What do you want me to say?' He leaned back in his chair and smiled humourlessly. 'Let me guess. How about, "Oh, of course, Nicole, if it bothers you I won't do it." ' The thin smile faded into a narrow-eyed scowl. 'Well, think again, lady. This is my cabin. I don't want you here, and the only thing that keeps me from throwing you out in the snow is my sense of humanity and common decency.'

'Decency!' she exploded. 'Humanity! Do you call making me sleep on that—that torture chamber over there decency?' She made a sweeping gesture with her arm towards the offending couch, knocking over her coffee-cup in the process. Ignoring it as it dripped into her lap, she continued her harangue. 'Or making me wash up your dirty dishes when I don't even know how? Or expecting me to...'

But her words were obviously falling on deaf ears. With one last puff of his cigarette he carefully stubbed it out in his plate. Then he picked up his notebook, rose to his feet and sauntered away from her over to his desk without a word or a backward glance.

He sat down with his back to her and began leafing through his charts. 'You'd better start heating some more water for the dishes,' he called to her over his shoulder after a few minutes. 'They're the only ones we have.'

The storm continued in earnest for what seemed like weeks, but which was actually only three days. By the second day, Nicole had just about given up hope of ever being rescued. Maybe by spring they'd send out a search party to look for her body.

She might just as well be dead, she thought gloomily as she gazed out of the window at the awful stuff that covered everything as far as the eye could see, filling the sky and weighing down the branches of the surrounding evergreens so that they bent over nearly to the ground.

Although the hostilities with Dirk Morgan had become less vocal, the war between them was still being waged on a powerful unspoken level. She soon realised that arguing with him or trying to appeal to his sense of chivalry was a total waste of time. If he had any finer qualities, he kept them well hidden, and she confined her silent opposition to performing the chores he assigned her as slowly, reluctantly and badly as possible. She wasn't his slave, after all, nor was she accustomed to having to do menial tasks.

He seemed to be taking the situation well in his stride, even though he had made no secret of his disgust at having to put up with her at all. He had a daily routine that he followed faithfully. He was always up and dressed by the time Nicole woke up in the morning, already cooking their breakfast. After the largely silent meal, he would go to his desk and work for an hour or two, then get up to tidy the cabin and sweep it clean. After lunch he would go outside to chop more firewood and bring it inside, then work at his desk again until it was time to cook their supper.

He also tinkered with the radio periodically, but apparently was making no headway in repairing it, because all Nicole ever heard from it was the crackle of static and a series of loud squawks. She'd given up asking him about it or urging him to get it working. He was as anxious for her departure as she was, and was doing all he possibly could to hasten it.

By the third day of the storm, it slowly began to dawn on her that her depressed mood was far more the result of boredom than it was overwork. The only recreation she had was playing endless games of patience with an old greasy deck of cards she'd found in the cupboard.

It was in the evening, after supper. Dirk was at his desk ignoring her as usual, and Nicole was sitting at the table after doing up the dishes, playing another boring game of cards. All of a sudden she couldn't stand it any longer, the confinement, the silence, the utter, mind-boggling boredom.

She jumped up from her chair, swept the playing cards off the table on to the floor and started pacing up and down the room, wringing her hands, groaning audibly and muttering to herself under her breath. When she reached his desk, Dirk was gazing up at her questioningly.

'I can't stand this another minute!' she cried. 'I'm going out of my mind! If you don't talk to me or do something, I'm going out that door——' she pointed dramatically '—and I'll start walking until I reach civilisation or freeze to death!'

'Believe me, it'll be freezing to death,' he said mildly.

'I don't care!' She put her hands on her hips and glared down at him, wild-eyed, on the verge of hysteria.

Dirk stared at her for several seconds. Then he nodded briefly, rose to his feet and put his hands on her shoulders, gripping them hard, as though to brace her. At his touch, Nicole felt a sudden rush of hot tears stinging behind her eyes. She shut then tight, forcing back the imminent sobs.

'OK,' he said softly, 'I guess you've had enough.'

She sniffled loudly and her eyes flew open. 'What do you mean?'

'I mean that for the whole time you've been here, the entire four endless days, I've been waiting for you to come down off your high horse and face reality. Now it looks as though you just might be ready.'

She wiped her eyes with the back of her hand and shook her head. 'I don't understand.'

Dirk dropped his hands from her shoulders and braced his hips back against the desk. 'Listen,' he explained, 'you barged in here like the lady of the manor, expecting me to wait on you, comfort you, even to entertain you, and it's just not going to be that way. We're stuck here together until someone can get through to take you back where you belong. Until then, we've both got to make the best of a bad situation.'

'What does that mean?' she asked suspiciously.

'It means that we both have to pull our own weight. Whether you believe it or not, I really do have important work here. It's actually more than one man can handle. Before you came, before that first storm that brought you here, I'd spent several weeks out in the field, tracking the animals I'm studying, gathering information about their hibernation patterns.' He shrugged. 'To tell you the truth, this storm is rather a blessing. It gives me time to organise my material and collate my findings.'

'Well, that's all well and good for you,' said Nicole. 'But it doesn't help me a whole lot. Can't you understand? I'm going out of my mind with sheer boredom——!' Her voice began to rise again.

'I'm coming to that,' he broke in. 'There's plenty you could do if you'd just quit feeling sorry for yourself long enough to look around you.'

'Oh, really?' she drawled sarcastically. 'Like what?'

He sighed and gestured impatiently with his hand. 'Like cleaning up the cabin. Like doing the cooking.' He gave her a grim sweeping look. 'Or getting yourself in better shape. You look like something the cat dragged in and discarded.'

Nicole stiffened, about to lash back at him, to tell him he wasn't exactly a model out of *Gentlemen's Quarterly* himself, but in the next moment she realised that what he was saying made sense.

She glanced down at herself. The ski pants were stiff by now with grime, her shirt wrinkled and dirty. She had rinsed out her underwear every morning and dried it in front of the fire while Dirk was out chopping wood, and each day she did wash her face, but that was about the extent of it.

That was nothing like the Nicole West she knew. Ordinarily the most meticulous of women, she had let herself go to pieces physically just as she was collapsing mentally. Dirk was right. She'd been behaving not only childishly and unrealistically, but downright destructively.

'Not only could you take the household burdens off me so I could get on with my work,' he went on, 'but you could help me with that too, if you wanted.' He shrugged diffidently. 'You might not find it the most fascinating subject in the world, but at least it would give you something to do.'

Nicole raised her eyes to see that he was smiling down at her, the first real smile he'd given her since her arrival. In his present mood, he seemed like a different person, much more human and approachable. And much more attractive. It was as though she was really seeing him for the first time, not as her enemy, but as a man.

As she gazed at him, she began to wonder how he would look without the heavy black beard and with his shaggy hair cut properly. He had fine eyes, deep green and speckled, a firm chin with a slight dent in it, and a strong, straight nose. The planes of his face hollowed down from high, prominent cheekbones, and when he smiled there were two deep clefts on either side of his thin firm mouth that were not quite dimples.

Finally she lowered her eyes. 'You might be right,' she murmured. 'I'll think about it.'

By the next morning the storm had passed over at last. When Nicole awoke to see the bright sunshine streaming through the window over the counter, it suddenly seemed like a brand new world.

She jumped off the couch, stretched widely, and ran over to the window. Dirk was just about to sit down at the table to eat his breakfast, and when she reached his side he turned to her and gave her another of those wonderful smiles.

'Looks like today might be the day,' he said. He pointed outside through the window. 'It finally quit snowing.'

'Yes, I saw,' she said happily. 'Isn't it marvellous?' Then she ran a hand through her tangled hair as it dawned on her how terrible she looked. 'Oh, lord!' she groaned. 'If I'm going to be rescued today, I'd better go try to get myself cleaned up.'

'I've heated you some water,' said Dirk, pointing at the stove. 'And you'll find some of my shirts and socks in the cupboard out in the washhouse. You'll swim in them, but they're clean, and you can help yourself if you like.'

'Thanks very much,' she said. 'That's very kind of you.'

He sat down at the table and picked up his fork. 'I'm going to go ahead and eat without you. Now that the weather has cleared, I have work to do out in the field and will probably be gone most of the morning. So take your time.'

'All right,' she said, and reached for the pan on the stove. 'I'll get my own breakfast later.'

'If you hear a helicopter going over,' he said, 'just go outside and stand in the clearing in front of the cabin and wave your arms like mad.'

'But will they see me?'

'Sure. A helicopter can fly quite low. And they'll be looking for you, remember?'

Nicole laughed. 'Yes, of course.'

When she stepped outside, she was immediately struck with the overpowering beauty of the scene around her. Everything was covered with a pristine white blanket of snow that sparkled dazzlingly in the sunshine. It actually was a new world, she thought as she picked her way slowly through the deep drifts towards the bathroom hut.

There was a small cracked mirror over the metal washbowl, which Nicole hadn't even bothered to glance at in the four days she'd spent trapped in this wilderness. Now, when she examined her reflection, she was appalled at how badly she had neglected her appearance.

Her long dark hair was a total disaster, the careful coiffure still pinned up haphazardly, but full of snarls. And she didn't even have a comb! She glanced around the tiny room. On the stand next to the washbowl Dirk's personal effects were laid out neatly, shaving gear, two clean toothbrushes, toothpaste, a comb and hairbrush, and several wrapped bars of soap. He'd said she could borrow some of his clothes. Maybe he wouldn't mind if she used his comb.

There was a wooden cupboard to the right that she had never bothered to inspect. Inside were clean towels and washcloths and a stack of neatly folded shirts and socks. A red shirt, she thought, so they'd be sure to see her.

Gritting her teeth, which were already chattering with cold, she quickly stripped off her dirty clothes and poured the pan of hot water into the bowl. For the next half-hour, shivering and shaking, she soaped and rinsed herself thoroughly, brushed her teeth, and washed her hair. Then she used the rapidly cooling water to soak her blouse, heavy stockings and underwear. She could dry them later in front of the fire.

By then she was freezing, her fingers and toes numb with cold. She'd done all she could. She wrapped one towel around her wet hair and had just started drying off with another, when she heard the faint sound of a motor off in the distance. She raised her head and cocked her ears, listening as it grew louder.

The helicopter! With a cry of relief, she stumbled over to the door, anxious to get outside and start signalling. Then she stopped short. She was not only stark naked, but barefoot as well. She couldn't possibly go out in the snow like that. Oh, lord, she thought in a panic. What shall I do?

'Boots!' she muttered aloud. 'Where are my boots?' If she could at least get them on her feet, it wouldn't be so bad. She could wrap a towel around herself, even slip on her jacket.

As she struggled to shove her bare feet inside the damp boots, the sound of the helicopter kept getting louder, until it seemed to be hovering directly overhead, the motor rumbling loudly in the silence of the forest, and she prayed that they wouldn't give up and leave before she could get outside.

But by the time she had managed to cram one foot even part way inside one boot, the engine was already growing fainter. She just stood there, shaking, fighting the sobs of sheer frustration welling up inside her, and for a moment she was strongly tempted to simply throw herself down on the floor, just like a child, and give in to the hopeless tears.

But something stopped her. She thought about Dirk's words last night. He was right: she had behaved badly and ended by hurting only herself. She had to calm down. If they came looking for her once, they'd come again. In the meantime, she'd just have to make the best of it, take Dirk's advice, and at least try to make herself useful.

She pulled on her ski pants and Dirk's red shirt. With a pair of dry socks on her feet, the boots slipped on easily. She was just about to leave when she noticed the used towel and washcloth lying on the floor where she had left them. She stooped down to pick them up. If she was going to pull her weight, she might as well start now.

Back in the warmth of the cabin, she hung her wet clothes in front of the fire and pulled Dirk's comb through her long wet hair, hoping he wouldn't object to her using it. When her hair was dry, she twisted it into a thick braid and went over to the counter to try to cook herself some breakfast.

She'd watched Dirk light the gas stove several times, but in her sulky mood had never really paid attention to how he did it, and she didn't want to blow up the cabin. She bent down to examine the burner more closely, and was just about to chance lighting a match to see if it would work when through the window she caught a glimpse of Dirk himself, striding through the snow towards the cabin. Now he could teach her how to fire the stove.

When he came inside, stamping the snow from his feet and taking off his heavy jacket and gloves, his face was glowing from the cold, his eyes sparkling, and Nicole could hardly believe how glad she was to see him.

'I heard the helicopter,' he said as he hung his coat up on the peg by the door. He came towards her, eyeing her carefully. 'I take it they didn't see you.'

'Afraid not. I was in the wash hut, starkers, and couldn't even get my boots on, much less any decent covering.' She had to smile at the memory. 'It was actually pretty funny!'

His eyes widened at her. 'I must say you're taking it well,' he commented drily.

She shrugged. 'Well, as you said yourself, I just have to make the best of a bad situation.' When he continued to stare, the smile faded from her lips. 'I'm sorry, Dirk,' she said stiffly. 'I realise quite well what a pest I've been and how anxious you are to be rid of me. I *did* try, you know.'

'I know,' he said gruffly. 'Never mind. They'll be back.'

Nicole hesitated a moment, debating inwardly before speaking, then made up her mind and plunged ahead. 'I just want to say that I'm also sorry for the way I've been acting. You were right— I've only been making a bad situation worse for both of us.'

He nodded briefly. 'OK. Let's just forget it. I have to admit I haven't exactly been a model host myself.' He gave her a grudging smile, then his eyes narrowed in frank appraisal. 'That shirt looks quite fetching on you. And I see you've done something about your hair. It looks nice.'

He turned from her then and started walking over to his desk. Nicole could only stare open-mouthed at his straight retreating back. Nice? A compliment? She could hardly believe her ears.

'Er—Dirk,' she called after him, 'would you mind teaching me how to work the stove?'

He turned around. 'No, not at all.' He came back and reached for the box of wooden matches sitting on the windowsill. 'It's really quite simple. Just watch carefully while I do it once, then you can try.'

He leaned over the stove, and she bent down beside him, her eyes fixed on his large, strong hands. They were so close that their heads were almost touching, and she could still smell the cold, clean, pungent scent of the outdoors that lingered on his hair and skin.

'The stove is powered with butane,' he explained. 'This handle controls the flow of the gas into the burner.' He turned it slowly. 'Give it about a quarter-turn, then light it.'

He struck a match and touched the flame to the burner. There was a slight puff as it caught into a low ring of fire, and Nicole involuntarily jumped. She gave Dirk a quick glance, but all his attention was concentrated on the job at hand, his eyes narrowed, a slight frown on his face.

'Then,' he went on, 'you can adjust the burner as high or low as you want. High for heating water, low for cooking.'

By then she had stopped paying attention to what he was saying or doing and just continued to stare at him. As the daughter of a rich and famous father, Nicole had met hundreds of men in her life, athletes, captains of industry, even a few movie stars. But none of them had affected her in quite the way this one had.

She compared him mentally to Victor Channing, the man her father was so intent on marrying her off to. They were probably about the same age, mid-thirties, but then all similarity stopped. Actually, in many ways Victor was the nicer of the two men. He'd always treated her with elaborate courtesy, anxious to please her, even a trifle subservient.

Dirk Morgan, on the other hand, was aggravating, dictatorial, hard to please and would never lift a finger to do her bidding. Yet there was an air about him that she found strangely appealing, even challenging, and she found herself trying to picture what he would look like without the beard.

Perhaps, like some men, he grew it to hide a weak jaw, or a receding chin. He had a nice mouth, though, wide and generous, with a thin upper lip, the lower one rather full. What she could see of his jaw looked firm enough, and the bone structure of his face was strong, with flat planes rising to high, prominent cheekbones.

All of a sudden she realised that he was gazing at her intently. As their eyes met, she caught a gleam in those flecked depths, a familiar unmistakable sign that told her he was aware of her for the first time as a woman instead of an annoyance. The wordless gaze held for just a few brief seconds, until, flushing, she looked away.

'I'm sorry,' she murmured. 'I was wool-gathering.'

Dirk straightened up, turned off the burner and handed her the box of matches. 'Here,' he said gruffly. 'You try it now.'

She took the matches from him, her hands shaking slightly, and tried to focus on what she was doing. As she stared blankly down at the stove, however, all she was aware of was Dirk's eyes still fastened on her. Mindlessly, she turned the handle, and immediately his hand clamped down firmly over hers.

'No!' he said. 'You're letting in too much gas.'

The hand remained on hers, warm and strong, then started moving, tentatively, almost impercep-tibly. Nicole turned to him, and once again their eyes locked together. She watched, mesmerised, as his head bent slowly towards her.

Then, suddenly, he dropped his hand, jerked himself upright and took a step back from her. 'Go on,' he prompted. 'Try it again.'

Really concentrating this time, Nicole followed his directions slowly and meticulously, until finally she had lit the burner properly. Exhilarated at her success, she straightened up and turned to him, smiling with delight.

'I did it!' she cried.

'Well, it's not exactly splitting the atom,' he commented drily. Then he thawed enough to give her a distant smile. 'But congratulations anyway.'

He turned from her then and strode across the room to his desk. Nicole stood there looking after him, hurt more than she would have believed possible at his sudden cool withdrawal, just when they seemed finally to have arrived at a friendly basis. Had she been mistaken about the moment they had shared? Did he find her repulsive in her dishevelled condition?

She grabbed the bucket and swept it angrily off the counter. He just didn't like her; he'd made that perfectly clear since the day she arrived. He thought she was useless, a spoilt brat who didn't know the first thing about taking care of herself or pulling her own weight under difficult conditions.

Well, she'd show him, she promised herself grimly as she stalked over to the door. She'd make herself so indispensable to him that, when she did leave, he'd be sorry to see her go!

CHAPTER THREE

ORDINARILY, Dirk got up before Nicole was even conscious, heated his water, and went out to the washhouse to bathe and dress. Then he would come back and cook breakfast while she was still sleeping. He was such a quiet man that, even though she was usually dimly aware of his movements in the cabin, it wasn't until after he left that she came fully awake.

The next morning, however, when she heard him at the stove heating water for his bath, she was immediately alert. She cocked an eye open and shifted her weight cautiously on the lumpy couch. Somehow it didn't seem nearly as uncomfortable now as it had at first. Either the broken springs had receded under her weight, or the contours of her body were beginning to conform to the lumps.

When she was sure Dirk was gone, she sat up, yawning and stretching. Through the window she could see the first early morning streaks of light shining faintly on the white snow, casting the inside of the cabin in a dusky half-light that was just enough to see by without having to light a lamp—another art she had yet to master.

She rose to her feet and ran her fingers through her long dark hair. Her elaborate coiffure was now a thing of the past, but at least it was clean. She'd braided it securely last night before going to bed, so that all she had to do was comb it out and tie a piece of string around it at the back of her neck.

Her decision to tackle more of the household chores was still fresh in her mind. Not only did it seem imperative to prove herself to Dirk somehow, but she had to do something to relieve the deadly boredom of the long days in the cabin. Last night in bed, she'd made up her mind to start by cooking their breakfast. It couldn't be that difficult, and now that she knew how to light the stove she was at least halfway there.

She groped her way over to the counter. It was much lighter here by the window, and she quickly assembled what she would need: frying-pan, bacon and eggs from the cooling cupboard, a can of orange juice, matches for the stove.

After almost singeing her eyebrows off twice with too high a flame, then not letting in nearly enough gas to get it lit at all, she finally arrived at the right combination, and she set the skillet on the nicely flaring burner.

Humming a little under her breath, she unwrapped the bacon and laid several strips in the pan. When it started to sizzle, she picked up the can of juice and was immediately baffled. How in the world did Dirk open cans? She pulled out the drawer under the counter to search for some kind of opener, but the light was still too dim to give her a clear view of the inside.

She tried to pull it out farther, but it seemed to be stuck. Exasperated, she finally gave it one good hard yank, and the next thing she knew the drawer was hanging empty in her hands, its contents rolling around on the floor at her feet.

With a muttered curse of frustration, Nicole got down on her hands and knees and fumbled around in the near-dark, anxious to get everything back in order before Dirk returned. Jabbing herself twice on a sharp-pointed object, she finally managed to retrieve what she hoped was everything that had fallen out.

With a sigh of relief, she lifted up the drawer and tried to slide it back in place. Once again it stuck, and it took several tries before she succeeded. She still hadn't found anything that remotely resembled a can-opener, but she couldn't worry about that now. There was a much more pressing problem confronting her.

She had been so intent on her struggles with the drawer that she hadn't even noticed the very suspicious odour until she had risen to her feet and was immediately engulfed in a cloud of black smoke.

The bacon! Flapping her arms around frantically in front of her, she finally managed to clear the air enough to see, and she gazed down in horror at the black, charred strips lying in the pan.

Quickly, without thinking, she grabbed hold of the hot handle with both hands, then dropped it instantly when a searing, burning sensation shot from her fingertips clear up her arm. She stood there groaning as the pan clattered to the floor.

'Damn, damn, damn!' she gritted through her teeth, shaking her stinging hands in the air.

She looked down to see that the skillet with its charred remnants was now overturned at her feet, and, what was worse, that in the whole process she had knocked the carton of eggs off the counter.

They now lay in a soggy broken mess alongside the pan.

Then from behind her came the sound of a very angry masculine voice. 'What the hell's going on here?'

She whirled around to see Dirk standing in the doorway, his long legs apart, the empty water bucket over one arm, his hands bunched into fists on his lean hips. His dark eyes were narrowed at her accusingly.

She opened her mouth, but not a word came out. All she could do was stand there staring at him, paralysed, the debris of her aborted breakfast lying smashed on the floor. Her hands felt like fire, but not for worlds would she let him see her even wince.

'I was fixing breakfast,' she finally managed to squeak out.

In three long strides he was beside her. He set the bucket on top of the counter, then stood staring down in stunned disbelief at the sticky, greasy mess at her feet.

He slowly raised his head. 'So I see,' he bit out tersely. 'May I ask how it happened to end up on the floor? Or is that your little culinary secret?'

Nicole eyed him warily. There was no point in hedging around, no way to salvage even a shred of dignity. She'd just have to come clean, tell him the unvarnished truth and throw herself on his mercy.

'Well, first the drawer spilled when I was looking for a can-opener—for the juice, you know. Then I noticed that the bacon was burning, and when I tried to pull the pan off the stove I didn't know it would be so hot, and when the eggs broke...'

Throughout her near-incoherent rambling re-
cital, Dirk's mouth had gradually begun to twitch
and the stern look to fade from his eyes. By the
time her voice trailed off, he was laughing openly.

'It's not funny!' she shouted. 'I really hurt
myself!'

She held out her hands, palms up. It was light
enough by now so that the angry red blisters that
had raised up on her skin were clearly visible. They
seemed to be swelling before her eyes.

'Oh!' she wailed tragically. 'My hands! Look at
them!'

Without a word, Dirk swung the water bucket
from the counter, marched over to the door and
opened it. He came back in a moment with a
bucketful of fresh snow and set it on the still-
flaming burner for a few seconds, just long enough
for it to melt. Then he shut the gas off and set the
bucket before her on the counter.

'Come on,' he said, grasping her forearms. 'Stick
your hands in the cold water. Best thing for burns.'

Squeezing her eyes shut and gritting her teeth,
Nicole did as she was told. The minute her stinging
hands hit the cool water the pain began to subside.
She breathed a sigh of relief.

'Here,' Dirk said after a few moments, 'let me
take a look.'

Obediently she raised her hands up out of the
water and held them out. Dirk grasped them gently
in his and bent his head down to examine her in-
juries more closely.

There was something very comforting about his
touch, which was far gentler than she would ever
have dreamed possible. He turned her hands over,

rubbing his thumbs lightly across the blisters in a slow, soothing motion that was almost erotic.

'I'm sorry, Dirk,' she said in a subdued voice. 'I was only trying to help.'

Still holding her hands, he raised his head to look at her. Their eyes met and held for a few seconds. He opened his mouth, as though to speak, then clamped it shut, a sudden scowl darkening his features.

'It's not serious,' he said gruffly. He dropped her hands and turned away. 'Better wear your gloves for a few days to keep the blisters from breaking. They're the best protection against infection.' He got down on his haunches and started clearing away the debris on the floor.

'I'm really sorry,' she said again. 'I really did want to make myself useful.'

'Listen,' he said, half snarling, 'if you want to help, the best thing you can do is stay out of my way.'

Nicole gazed down at his dark head, her lip quivering, the tears threatening again. Her hands still hurt, her clothes and hair were a mess, she was hungry and bored, and worst of all, she was stuck indefinitely out here in the wilderness with a man who detested her.

She walked slowly over to the couch and sat down in front of the fire, staring numbly into the flames. She could hear Dirk behind her, cleaning up the mess she had made. With her burned hands, she couldn't even do that much. After a while she could smell a fresh lot of bacon cooking in the pan. Properly, this time.

What was she going to do? What *could* she do? Everything she tried failed miserably and only seemed to push Dirk further away from her, made him resent her more than he already did.

Well, she vowed, setting her jaw firmly, she'd just have to try again. She'd *make* him admit she was more help than hindrance before she left that cabin, or die in the attempt!

That day marked a turning point in Nicole's attitude, and her relationship with Dirk began to change in subtle ways, at least as far as she was concerned. He remained pretty much the same, polite but distant, totally engrossed in his work. In fact, now that it was no longer snowing, he spent most of each day out in the field, tracking his animals or whatever it was he did.

She had been at the cabin for almost two weeks now, and, although she kept listening for the sound of a helicopter or some sign that someone was searching for her, she wasn't nearly as anxious to be rescued as she had been when she first came. By now they had probably given up on her anyway, assumed she'd perished in the storm, and as the days passed this troubled her less and less.

As soon as her hands healed, she gradually began to take on most of the responsibility for cooking and keeping the cabin clean, and she grew more confident with each small task conquered. Not only did this relieve the deadly boredom, but she soon found to her surprise that she actually enjoyed making herself useful. For the first time in her life, she had a purpose other than pleasing herself, and she even began to look back on her old life with distaste.

No matter how hard she tried, however, she couldn't get anything remotely resembling a compliment out of Dirk. Granted she still made an occasional mistake, which he was only too happy to point out to her, but by now she had become fairly efficient at the daily chores, relieving him of so much drudgery that he had more time to spend on his project.

But did he appreciate it? The most she ever got out of him was a thin, grudging smile, and not criticising her seemed to be as close to gratitude as he intended to get. Day by day her resentment grew. Each time he merely grunted when she served up a meal that wasn't burned, or managed to clean the cabin without knocking over his precious charts, the urge to shout at him or slap him grew stronger, anything to get some response out of him.

Yet her very anger drove her on to greater heights of accomplishment, to force him into an admission that she was helping him, and, now that she had the bare necessities under fair control, she began to look for things above and beyond the call of duty.

One morning after Dirk had left for the fieldwork that he found so entrancing, she noticed that the normally neat man had left two soiled shirts lying on his bed, probably planning to wash them later. Since all she had to wear besides Dirk's enormous shirt were the clothes she had arrived in, she had to wash them every day, usually after she had bathed, and she decided to surprise him by doing up the shirts at the same time.

In fact, while she was at it she might as well see if he had anything else that needed laundering. He kept his personal belongings in a large metal foot-locker beside his desk. It wouldn't hurt anything to take a quick look inside. She had no intention of prying. Still, she hesitated, and stood there staring at the locker across the room as though it might explode any minute.

She debated silently for a while longer, then said aloud, 'Why not?' It was worth the risk to impress him at last with her efficiency.

Feeling a little like a sneak thief, she practically tiptoed over to the locker and raised the lid. Sure enough, sitting right on top was Dirk's cotton laundry bag, obviously full. Nicole lifted it out and was just about to close the lid when a small leather-bound volume lying underneath caught her eye.

It looked to be some kind of address book. Would it hurt just to take one quick peep? She was dying of curiosity, as though learning the names and addresses of his friends and business associates might give her a clue to the man himself. She stared down at it, fighting temptation.

Glancing around guiltily, she reached down with one finger and flipped the pages of the book at random. It fell open at the letter S. There, in Dirk's neat, straight draughtsmanlike handwriting, was a list of names. As she glanced down it, she could see that there were two kinds of entries, one with complete names and addresses, the other with women's first names, followed by just the name of a town.

'Sandra,' she read, and after it 'San Francisco' and a telephone number. 'Sherry, Boston. Sylvie, Paris.'

Nicole couldn't tear her eyes from it. She was sorely tempted to explore the rest of the book, but by now her conscience was nagging at her, warning her she'd already gone too far. Quickly she shut the book, placed the laundry bag on top of it, and re-fastened the locker.

As she heated the washing water, she mulled over her discovery of that fabled 'little black book'. So he wasn't a monk! Somehow that fact considerably altered her view of him, from stern, dedicated scientist to a man who obviously had his pick of women. Still, his sex life wasn't any of her business, and she'd just have to put it out of her mind.

She turned to the task at hand, scrubbing the shirts vigorously for several minutes. If she wanted to impress him, they'd have to be *very* clean, much cleaner than *he* could get them. When she was through, she hung them on the line strung up in front of the blazing fire so they'd be dry before he got back. She could hardly wait to see the look on his face when he saw them.

She was just opening cans to start their evening meal when Dirk came back late that afternoon. As she listened to his footsteps outside stamping off the snow on his boots, her heart started to hammer with pleased anticipation. She wouldn't say anything, she decided. She wanted him to notice the shirts all by himself.

The door opened, and he came inside, his face red with cold. He took off his gloves, his heavy jacket and boots, then slipped his feet into his moccasins and started to cross over to the fire.

'Looks as though another storm is brewing,' he commented. 'I'd better make sure we have plenty of firewood. We don't want to get caught——'

He stopped in mid-sentence. He's noticed the shirts, Nicole thought, and couldn't resist a sideways glance to see his reaction to her surprise. He was standing there, staring at them, scratching his head, a puzzled look on his face.

'What the hell?' he said, and darted her a malevolent glance.

The modest smile Nicole had all prepared faltered and faded. Something was wrong. She glanced at the shirts, still hanging where she'd left them. They seemed all right to her. Was he annoyed that she'd finally proved to him just how useful she could be? She took another look. They *did* seem different. Were they possibly a little smaller than when she'd started out?

Dirk had whirled around and was pointing his finger at her. 'You washed them,' he stated flatly, making it sound very much like an accusation.

'Yes,' she replied brightly. 'I hope you don't mind, but I thought since I——'

'You used hot water!' he broke in, his voice rising with each syllable.

'Well, yes,' she said defensively. 'I wanted to get them extra clean.'

'Look at them!' He was almost shouting by now. 'Don't you know hot water shrinks woollens? How can anyone be so stupid?' He just stood there glaring at her. 'Hell,' he muttered disgustedly, 'it takes me days to teach you how to heat water, and look what it led to. I've created a monster!'

Hot tears of self-pity stung behind Nicole's eyes. She didn't even care at this point, and just let them spill over until they were pouring unchecked down her cheeks. She couldn't speak. Her eyes were so blurred that all she could see was that towering, menacing figure, virtually quivering with indignation. What would he do? Turn her out in the snow?

'Well, I'm sorry!' she finally managed to blubber. 'I was only trying to help.' She spread her hands wide in a dramatic gesture of defeat. 'What does it take to please you?' she cried.

She buried her face in her hands and turned away, sobbing openly now, tears of real despair. She almost wished he would turn her out in the snow. Her situation was hopeless. She was trapped here for heaven knew how long with a man who despised everything about her.

Suddenly she became aware of a presence behind her, a hand on her shoulder. Angrily she shrugged it off with a jerk, but it was back instantly, this time with a firmer pressure.

'Nicole,' came Dirk's low voice.

'What?' she bawled. 'What did I do wrong now?' She gave a loud sniffle.

'I'm sorry, Nicole,' he said. 'Please don't cry. I can't stand to hear a woman cry.'

'Well, that's too bad,' she snapped. She wiped her eyes with the back of her hand. 'You're the one who caused it.'

Both hands were on her shoulders now, kneading gently. His tall, strong body was pressed close to hers. Gradually the hurt and anger began to leak away, and she relaxed back against him with a deep sigh.

His head bent close to hers. 'Listen, Nicole,' he went on. 'I was only teasing.'

That did it. 'Teasing!' she cried. She pulled away and whirled around to face him. 'If you call that teasing, I must say you have a very perverted sense of humour! You were furious with me, and you know it!'

He set his jaw in a firm line and stared down at the floor for a moment, as though inwardly debating. When he raised his head again, there was a new look in his dark green eyes, a softer look that held a trace of mute appeal.

'All right,' he said at last, 'I admit it. I've behaved rather badly to you recently.'

'Badly?' Nicole cried. 'Recently?' She narrowed her eyes at him. 'You've resented me and treated me like some kind of pestilence from the moment I came.' The tears began to well up anew. 'Oh,' she groaned, wringing her hands, 'why didn't you just leave me out in the storm that day?'

'Come on, now,' Dirk said in a worried voice. 'Don't start crying again.' He reached out a hand and took her gently by the arm. 'Let's go over by the fire and sit down. I'll try to explain a few things.'

He led her over to the mangy couch. The offending shirts were still hanging in front of the fire, but by tacit consent they both averted their eyes from them.

When they were seated, Dirk at one end, Nicole as far away from him as she could get, he thought a moment, then turned to her, one arm resting on the back of the couch.

'I take it,' he began in a dry tone, 'that we're both agreed on one thing. I haven't exactly treated you like an honoured guest.'

Crossing her arms tightly in front of her, she nodded vigorously. 'Agreed,' she said tersely. 'Although I'd put it in somewhat stronger terms. You've behaved like a selfish, thoughtless, inconsiderate brute.'

'All right, have it your way,' he agreed reluctantly. 'Although you'll have to admit that at first you did rather come on as lady of the manor, blithely assuming I was going to wait on you hand and foot.'

When she opened her mouth to argue that point, he raised a hand to stop her. 'But we won't quibble. I just want to assure you that I don't ordinarily treat women like that, and ask you to try to see it from my point of view.'

'Oh, I know all about that,' she drawled, rolling her eyes. 'I disturbed your precious work.'

'No!' he snapped. 'That isn't it. Now, do you suppose you can keep quiet for five seconds and let me say what I've got on my mind, or shall we just forget it?'

'Sorry,' Nicole bit out tersely. 'Please continue.'

'What I'm trying to say is that this is a very awkward situation.' To her amazement, his face went up in flame. 'I mean,' he went on, 'you're a very beautiful woman, and I have all a man's normal instincts. We're all alone here. It could get sticky. I guess in an effort to avoid any—any——'

He waved a hand helplessly in the air. 'I just over-reacted,' he finished up lamely.

Nicole goggled at him, so astounded at this un-expected revelation that she was speechless. It threw an entirely new light on their whole relationship, and her head whirled in confusion. The one thought she clung to was that Dirk thought she was beauti-ful. That must mean he was attracted to her, had been from the very beginning, and had deliberately kept his distance to avoid temptation.

'In any event,' he was saying, 'I want you to know I do appreciate what you've done here, and that I admire the way you've adjusted to a bad situ-ation. What I don't know,' he went on glumly, 'is how in the hell to handle it.'

For the first time, Nicole felt that she was in control, that Dirk was the one at a disadvantage. Clearly, from now on, the status of their relation-ship was going to be up to her. She leaned back and gave him a long cool look.

'Well, Dirk,' she said in a firm, reasonable tone, 'since we're two mature, responsible adults, I see no reason why we can't get along on a friendly basis without getting into any—er—any—sticky situ-ation. After all, we don't know how long we'll be marooned here together, and I think the only sen-sible thing to do is to try to co-operate, to treat each other civilly, until I can get out of here.'

Even as she spoke, however, she was looking at him with new eyes, suddenly and intensely aware of him as a man. It simply had never dawned on her that he found her in the least appealing. Now she noticed things about him she never had before, how broad his shoulders were, how thick and crisp the dark hair, the interesting dark flecks in his green eyes. Even the beard didn't seem nearly so daunting.

'Well, that's all right, then,' he said cautiously. He rose to his feet and gave the shrunken shirts on the line one wry glance. 'And thanks for trying with the shirts.' He cocked an eyebrow at her and smiled. 'At least now you'll have something to wear that will fit you!'

Although the atmosphere was somewhat strained at dinner that night, after the new ground that had been broken in their little talk, Nicole felt better about her presence in Dirk's cabin than she ever had before, and by time they were halfway through with the meal they were chatting together amiably.

'Tell me,' he said over coffee, 'just how did you come to get lost in the storm that day? I have the feeling there's more to it than simply straying off the path out of idle curiosity.'

Nicole smiled wryly. 'To tell you the truth, I was running away. I was angry at my father, and wanted to brood a while by myself. I went too far, and then when the storm came up so suddenly I couldn't find my way back to the path.'

'He must have done something pretty terrible to make you do such a foolish thing.'

She shrugged. 'It seemed terrible at the time.' It couldn't hurt anything to tell him now. 'He was trying to push me into marrying a business associate of his, a man who could help him a lot. I didn't want to marry him. Father kept insisting. Finally, I just had enough.'

'Couldn't you just have told him you didn't want to marry this guy? This isn't the Dark Ages, you know.'

'Well, that sounds simple enough, but you'd have to know more about my background, the way I was brought up, to understand why I reacted the way I did.'

He leaned back in his chair and lit a long thin cigar. 'Why don't you tell me about it, then?'

'Well, I guess you could say I was raised with a silver spoon. You know, big house in Beverly Hills, servants, charge accounts, all the advantages of the idle rich. I never had a job, never had to do anything for myself.' She laughed. 'I never even learned how to drive. Dad always had a chauffeur, and he was at my disposal whenever I wanted to go somewhere.'

'Sounds great to me,' he said with feeling. 'Most of us have to scramble for every penny.'

'Yes, I guess it does sound great. But I see now that what it did was turn me into a helpless baby. As you so colourfully put it, a spoilt brat, who didn't even know how to boil water. I only began to realise that after I landed here and you *made* me pull my weight. I'll always be grateful to you for that, Dirk, no matter what happens.'

Their eyes met across the table, and suddenly the thought of the address book in Dirk's locker leapt into Nicole's mind. Who were those women?

'Anyway,' she went on hurriedly, dropping her eyes, 'when Father started pushing me into marrying Victor, I simply saw red. He'd never denied me anything before in my life, never made one demand on me. Now he was trying to make me do something that was utterly hateful to me.'

'I take it you're not too fond of this Victor,' he said carefully.

'Oh, Victor's all right,' she replied with a shrug. 'I just don't want to marry him. Actually, I've never wanted to marry at all. I used to think it was because I just hadn't met the right man, and in a way I was looking for him, waiting for him to come along. Now, after being here and having to make myself useful, I think the real reason was that I needed to find out first who I was and what I could do.'

'Well then, it hasn't been a total waste, has it?' he asked lightly.

'No. Not from my point of view anyway.'

He stubbed out his cigar carefully in the little metal ashtray by his plate, then rose to his feet. He yawned and stretched widely, and as Nicole watched him strange sensations began to flutter around the vicinity of her heart, a warmth that hovered dangerously on the edge of desire.

Once again she wondered what he would look like without the heavy beard, and before she could stop herself she'd blurted it out. 'Do you always wear that beard?' she asked.

'No, not always. It's more convenient out here in the wild not to have to shave.' He grinned at her. 'Besides, it keeps my face warm. I shave it off every year when I go back to the civilised world.'

'What is your world, Dirk?' she asked. 'I mean, what exactly is it you do?'

'At the moment, I teach wildlife biology at Stanford part of the year. My field research is funded by grants.'

'Where do you live?'

'I have an apartment in San Francisco, just up the peninsula from the university, but I have to do so much travelling in my work that I'm not there a lot.'

'Are you married?'

His eyes widened in something like horror. 'Hell, no!' he exclaimed with feeling. Then, more calmly, he added, 'I have nothing against marriage, but with the kind of work I do I'm confronted with a pretty clear choice. I could never do justice to a wife, a home, a family, the way I have to live.'

'Other men do it,' Nicole commented.

'Well, if it comes to that, other spoilt rich girls get married too. It's all a matter of individual choice.'

'Yes,' she agreed, 'you're probably right.'

Dirk hesitated a moment, then said, 'Listen, maybe you'd be interested in helping me with my work. Now that you've got the housework under such expert control, it must get boring here all day by yourself, and I could use the help.'

'Why, yes,' she replied immediately, pleased, 'I'd like that very much.'

CHAPTER FOUR

THE next morning, however, when Dirk elaborated a little more on the details of his work, Nicole wasn't quite so certain she'd made the wisest decision in the world. This year, he told her, his primary field of interest was the enormous and lethal grizzly bears that roamed free in the park.

As she listened to him explain over breakfast how he tracked the animals, the long hours he spent observing their hibernation and feeding patterns, the more sober she became.

'I don't know, Dirk,' she said dubiously when he had finished. 'I'm not so sure I want to fool around with bears. I've never even seen a wild animal outside a zoo. Isn't it awfully dangerous?'

'It can be,' he said. 'Grizzlies in particular are extremely unpredictable. Ordinarily, they won't bother you unless you startle them or challenge them in some way, but the ironclad rule is, never take a chance. A full-grown grizzly can kill a man with one swipe of a paw. And never, ever, under any circumstances, get between a mother bear and her cubs.' He swallowed the last of his coffee and rose from the table. 'But when I asked if you wanted to help me, I wasn't thinking of your coming with me out in the field.'

'Oh,' Nicole said, breathing a sigh of relief, 'that's good.'

'To tell you the truth,' he went on with a smile, 'you'd only be a hindrance to me.' He held up a hand. 'No offence. It's just that it's really a one-man job. What I had in mind was showing you how I code the data I collect so that you can enter it in the log. That would save me a lot of time.'

He was actually going to trust her with his precious charts and notebooks! 'Fine,' she said. 'I'd like to give it a try.'

He stood looking down pensively at her. 'However, I do think it would do you good to get out more than you do, as long as you're stuck here. It's really beautiful country. I have an extra pair of snowshoes you could use if you'd like to explore around a little.'

She bit her lip and looked up at him uncertainly. 'Well, I might give it a try,' she said slowly. 'If you're sure it's safe.'

Dirk put a reassuring hand on her shoulder. 'About all you'll see around here are small harmless animals like squirrels or beavers. Bears rarely come near human habitations unless there's food lying around—that's why I'm so careful about burying our garbage.' He gave her shoulder a little squeeze, then dropped his hand. 'You'll be all right. Just don't stray too far from the cabin.'

Nicole laughed nervously. 'If you say so.'

He went over to the door to put on his jacket and boots, then stooped over to strap on his snowshoes. 'You keep the home fires burning,' he said, buttoning his heavy jacket. 'And when I get back tonight I'll show you how I enter my data in the log.'

He opened the door, gave her a little salute, and went outside. She hurried over to the window and watched him as he slung his pack over his shoulders and ploughed off across the snow towards the thicket of tall trees beyond the clearing.

When he was out of sight she was suddenly struck with a powerful sense of isolation. She'd never felt so alone. After their talk last night, she felt closer to Dirk Morgan, a virtual stranger, than she ever had to another human being. Although there had always been a lot of people in her life, even a few tepid romances to look back on, all her past relationships now seemed somewhat superficial in comparison.

Not only did she sense more depth to this man than her other friends, and a deeper commitment to his work, but he had treated her from the beginning like a responsible adult rather than a painted doll. Even what she once thought of as his cruel treatment she now saw was his way of making her face reality, assume real obligations.

She was also very flattered that he wanted her to help him with his work. It was a heady experience to be needed, and the prospect of another long boring day in the cabin all by herself was profoundly depressing. Still, she had the evening to look forward to, and as she cleaned up the breakfast things she decided to take Dirk's advice and explore a little outside the cabin.

When the last dish was done, the burner safely turned off, she put on her heavy jacket, boots and gloves and opened the cabin door. It was a cold, crisp morning, with the snow sparkling brightly under a cloudless blue sky. She stood there for a moment, hesitating and gazing around at the strikingly beautiful scene, the snow-covered clearing, with Dirk's tracks still visible, the tall stand of evergreens at the edge of it, then mile after mile of mountainous country beyond.

She drew in a deep lungful of the fresh crisp air, and was just about to step outside when she heard the motor.

She pricked up her ears. The rough chopping sound grew louder with each passing second. The helicopter had come back! They *were* still searching for her! Nicole stood in the doorway for a moment, listening, all poised to run out into the clearing and start waving. She didn't want to miss them this time.

But before she could take one step, something stopped her. It was as though an invisible hand was holding her back against her will. Once she left here, she would go back to her old existence, the long, idle days of shopping and luncheons, the boring round of parties, the squabble with her father over marrying Victor.

Then she knew. She didn't *want* to be rescued! She wanted to stay here with Dirk. For the first time in her life she felt as though she was good for something besides indulging her own whims. She couldn't give that up, not yet.

Then she sobered, thinking of her father, of the worry and pain she was causing him. But he was the one who had driven her to it, with his pigheaded insistence that she marry Victor. For all his indulgence of her, he had never shown her any real understanding or affection. In fact, all the material things he had showered on her could well have been a substitute for the affection he couldn't show, perhaps didn't feel.

Still, that was no excuse for putting him through the grief of losing his only child. But would he grieve? What had she ever been to him but a doll to be pampered, a means to an end, a pawn in his own calculated ambition for power? It wouldn't be forever. She'd have to leave eventually. Dirk himself would be going in the spring.

As the sound of the motor grew louder, however, she knew she couldn't do it. It would be too cruel. No matter how deficient he had been as a parent, he was still her father, and she at least owed him the knowledge that she was safe.

She stepped out into the clearing and waited, dreading what was coming. As the seconds passed, her heart grew heavier and heavier at the thought of leaving this serene, beautiful place, leaving Dirk.

Then, all of a sudden, she realised that the engine sound was gradually receding. She could have shouted aloud for joy. Maybe they hadn't even been looking for her, or maybe they'd given up searching in the vicinity of the cabin, and were trying other areas of the vast forest. In any event, she was safe for a while. She could stay with a clear conscience.

That night after their evening meal, Nicole and Dirk sat side by side at his desk, their heads close together, while he explained to her what it was he wanted her to do.

'You see how I've colour-coded the entries,' he said, pointing to the log book. 'Each colour represents a different area of the park, and I enter the animal sightings within them by date.'

Nicole tried to pay attention, but she was actually only half listening to him. The fire was crackling behind them, the room was warm and cosy, and she was intensely, almost painfully, aware of the nearness of him. They were so close that it seemed she could almost hear his heart beat.

She watched the way he held his pencil in his strong capable hands, the palms callused over from the heavy work he did each day, the thick dark hair that fell over his forehead, the movement of the wonderful mouth as he spoke. Even the beard didn't seem nearly so intimidating as it used to. His instructions were clear and to the point, his voice low, matter-of-fact, and she loved listening to its deep cadences.

'Well,' he said at last, leaning back in his chair and turning to her, 'any questions?'

She glanced over at him. 'No, I don't think so. It seems clear enough.'

'Think you can handle it, then?'

She nodded. 'Yes.'

'Good. If you could give it an hour or two every day it would save me a lot of time.' He smiled crookedly, the deep green eyes gleaming, and when he spoke his voice was teasing. 'I might even be talked into playing a game of cards with you in the evening as a reward. How are you at gin rummy?'

'Oh, a demon!' she said with a laugh.

Dirk shoved his chair back. 'All right, you're on.' He rose to his feet. 'Why don't you get the cards out, and I'll make some coffee?'

Nicole stared down at her hands, hesitating. Ever since he had come back late that afternoon she had debated telling him about the helicopter. Somehow the fact that she hadn't *wanted* them to find her made her feel guilty, as though her very wish had kept them away.

'What is it?' he asked finally. 'Afraid I'll skunk you?'

She looked up at him and cleared her throat. 'Dirk, I heard the helicopter again today.'

His expression grew suddenly grave. 'I know.' He sat back down and leaned towards her. 'I heard it too. I'm sorry, Nicole. I knew they'd missed the cabin. I guess when they didn't spot you here the last time they gave up and went on to search other areas. It's a big park.'

She didn't know what to say. What she wanted to tell him was that she was glad they'd missed her, glad she could stay with him a while longer, but she didn't quite have the nerve.

'I am sorry,' he said again. 'I know how anxious you are to get back to civilisation.'

She laughed lightly. 'Not half as anxious, I'll bet, as you are to be rid of me!'

He cocked an eyebrow and gave her a slow grin. 'Oh, I don't know about that. I'm getting rather used to having you around. Especially now that I'm getting some work out of you. Think of all the things I'll have to do for myself when you leave.'

'Have I really been a help, Dirk?' she asked eagerly, leaning a little closer to him so that their shoulders just touched.

Immediately his face darkened and he drew back from her abruptly. 'Don't do that!' he snapped.

Nicole widened her eyes at him. 'What? What did I do?'

'You know quite well,' he said gruffly.

She leaned back in her chair and stared at him. Did he find her repulsive? She had no make-up, she was lucky to keep her hair clean and combed, and she swam even in one of Dirk's shrunken shirts.

'Well,' she said with a nervous laugh, 'I realise I wouldn't win any beauty contests, but——'

'That's not it,' he broke in abruptly.

'Well, what then? I know we got off to a bad start, but I thought we were finally beginning to get along rather well.'

The dark eyes bored into her for a long moment before he spoke again. Then he sighed and waved a hand in the air. 'Do you have any idea how hard it's been for me to keep my distance from you these past few weeks?' His voice was low, full of a throbbing intensity.

A flood of warm relief washed over her. It wasn't distaste after all. In fact, it sounded very much like desire!

'Why, Dirk?' she asked softly. 'Why keep a distance?'

His eyes flew open at that, then narrowed. 'Wait a minute. Do you know what you're saying?'

As a matter of fact, she didn't. Now that it was out in the open, she was filled with confusion. Some deep, dark instinct had emboldened her to ask the question, a question she now realised must have sounded very provocative.

'Well, I didn't mean...' she faltered, and shrugged helplessly. 'I guess what I really meant was that I like you, and I'm glad you like me.'

Dirk gave her a wry smile. 'Well, unless you have something more on your mind than friendship, I think we'd better keep it at that.' Then the smile faded and his expression grew serious. 'I told you once I thought you were a very beautiful woman. We're here all alone. I think you know what that could mean, where it could lead.'

He continued to gaze at her, this time with an ineluctable question in his eyes. Nicole's mind raced. His meaning was quite clear. He was telling her that he wanted her.

She didn't know what to say. She knew by now how attracted she was to him, that there was nothing she'd like more than to feel his arms around her, his face next to hers, his mouth——

'Come on,' he said, breaking into her thoughts. He got up again and started walking away. 'Get out the cards,' he called over his shoulder. 'I think I'll have a drink!'

From then on the days passed more quickly. Not only was Nicole becoming more involved all the time in Dirk's project as she understood it better, but she did manage to explore a little further each day outdoors after Dirk had taught her how to manoeuvre on the extra pair of snowshoes.

She was quite content with her situation, even happy, and dreaded the thought that one day it would have to end. Each time she heard Dirk tinker with the broken radio, a cold chill gripped her, and she prayed he'd never get it fixed.

She had been at the cabin for over a month now, and, after the violent storm in her first week here, they had enjoyed weeks of uninterrupted fine weather. It was still cold enough so that the heavy blanket of snow remained frozen, but the sun shone brightly every day, and Dirk chopped enough firewood to keep the inside of the cabin warm.

Nicole usually did her household chores and made Dirk's log entries in the morning after he left, then after lunch would spend a few hours in the afternoon out of doors until he returned. By now she had ventured almost as far away as the edge of the clearing, a distance of some five hundred feet, and, although Dirk had firmly forbidden her to feed any of the small animals, she loved watching the squirrels and chipmunks scamper along the tallest branches of the trees, scolding her for invading their territory in their strange, squeaky growls.

Today she had decided to go into the forest itself, beyond the clearing, just a few feet at first, to get a closer look at the animals. She had caught a glimpse of what looked like a racoon a few days ago, and was eager to get a closer look at the roly-poly creatures with the big black circles around their eyes. Dirk had said they were quite harmless, even friendly.

The sun set early in the mountains, especially this late in the year, and by the time she had bundled herself up in her heavy outdoor clothing and boots there would only be another few hours of daylight. That meant Dirk would be back soon.

Once outside, she half trudged, half slid awkwardly on the snowshoes towards the tall stand of fir trees at the edge of the clearing. It was warmer now than it had been in the morning, with the sun reflecting brightly on the snow, a slight breeze blowing, and the air clean and fresh.

It was slow going through the deep crusty snow, and by the time she reached the first tree Nicole was more than ready to turn around and go back. There was no sign of the raccoon.

Besides that, she was beginning to feel distinctly uneasy. It was the first time she had been this far from the cabin, and the tremendous sweep of forest and snow-covered mountains that surrounded her filled her with an awed sense of her own littleness and vulnerability and isolation.

As she plodded back towards the cabin, her head down against the quickening breeze, suddenly in her peripheral vision she caught a glimpse of something moving. Alarmed, she raised her head. Just ahead and off to one side were two bear cubs, frolicking in the snow. She stopped short and stood there quite still, watching them as they played, batting their paws at each other and rolling around together on the ground awkwardly in the snow.

She wasn't quite sure what to do. They certainly didn't *look* dangerous. They were only babies, mere teddy bears, cute little bundles of furry energy. As she watched them, she suddenly recalled Dirk's warning: never get between a mother bear and her cubs.

Quickly she scanned the area. There was no sign of the mother, but prudence dictated that she take no chances, and she started moving again cautiously towards the cabin.

At her first step, she heard a low rumble coming from behind her. She stopped dead in her tracks, paralysed, afraid to move forward, afraid to turn around. Slowly, with aching anxiety, she inched her head around until out of the corner of her eye a dark shape loomed.

Her heart simply stopped beating. It was a very large, very angry-looking, full-grown bear, up on its hind legs, huge and hulking, its beady eyes fixed on her. Nicole stifled the scream that rose in her throat. Don't startle them, Dirk had said. Don't challenge them. Just walk away quietly and calmly.

But even as she raised a foot to take the first tentative step, shaking violently in her boots, the bear let out another low menacing growl and moved towards her. Nicole closed her eyes. Her head spun dizzily. She was certain in the next moment the bear would lunge at her.

Then, dimly, she heard a voice, Dirk's voice, calling to her. She opened her eyes. He was standing just beyond the clearing in the shadow of the trees.

'Keep away from the cabin, Nicole,' he was saying in a low reassuring tone. 'And don't take one step towards the cubs. Don't even look at them. Stand right where you are. Do you understand? Just nod your head.'

Dumbly she nodded. She couldn't have moved if she'd wanted to. She kept her eyes fixed on Dirk. But what could he do? Did he have a gun? She didn't think so.

'Now,' he went on in the same calm voice, 'start walking towards me. But slowly, very slowly. Don't look at the mother bear and don't look at her cubs. Just walk away from them. It'll be all right. She won't bother you once she sees you're not interested in her cubs. Come on, now. One step.'

Stiffly, she finally managed to take the first rigid step.

'Good,' Dirk called. 'Now another. Come on! That's the way. Good girl! One more now.'

She kept on, her eyes squeezed tight now, following the sound of his voice, the constant low stream of encouraging instructions, until finally she felt his hands pulling her forward that last step. She sank up against him with a low moan of relief. Still shaking from head to foot, she threw her arms around his neck and buried her head in his shoulder.

Safe at last in Dirk's strong, sheltering arms, after several long minutes Nicole felt her panic gradually subsided into an occasional deep involuntary shudder. Still clinging to him with all her might, she finally was able to lift her head and gaze up at him.

The tenderness and concern she saw in his eyes was almost enough to make her forget the terrible danger they were in. He put a hand on her cheek and gave her a reassuring smile.

'It's OK now,' he said. 'They're gone.'

'All of them?' she croaked.

He nodded, the smile broadening. 'Yep. Mama too.' He gave a low chuckle of amusement. 'I wish you could have seen her bat those cubs around when she caught up with them! Mother bears are very loving and fiercely protective of their young, but great disciplinarians as well. No "Spare the rod and spoil the child" for them!'

'Dirk, it's not funny!' she exclaimed. 'I don't see how you can laugh. We could have been killed!'

'Well, we weren't, were we?' Keeping one arm around her shoulders, he hugged her to him. 'Come on, we can go back to the cabin now. They're long gone.'

Reluctantly, Nicole allowed him to lead her across the clearing, leaning against him heavily, stumbling along, still so shaken she couldn't have taken one step on her own, unable to breathe easily again until they were actually safe inside the cabin with the door shut.

However, the minute Dirk dropped his arm from her shoulder and started to take off his jacket, she was seized with a sudden attack of anxiety. Now that it was all over, the hard knot of fear in her stomach began to bubble up into a wave of hysteria. She clenched her fists at her sides and squeezed her eyes shut, fighting the waves of unreasoning panic that swept over her.

Half choking with the effort, she finally let out one strangled sob and broke into tears. She could feel herself going out of control as the sobs gradually began to turn into a weird kind of uncontrollable laughter, but she couldn't stop herself.

The next thing she knew, Dirk's hands were digging into her shoulders and he was shaking her, harder and harder, so that she could almost hear her teeth rattle. Gradually she began to snap out of it, and, with the tears still pouring down her face, she quieted down at last.

When her teeth had stopped chattering and her insides settled into place, she gave a loud sniffle and gazed up at Dirk. The look of deep concern on his face gave rise to a fresh bout of weeping, but this time they were tears of relief. Exhausted from the emotional trauma she'd been through, she closed her eyes and leaned into his strong embrace, throwing her arms around his waist and holding on to him for dear life as her one source of security.

'Oh, Dirk,' she mumbled against his chest, 'I was so frightened!'

He smoothed her hair back from her forehead. 'Of course you were,' he murmured soothingly. 'You had every right to be.'

His rough cheek was against hers, and his words came soft and warm in her ear. She heaved a deep sigh. Her eyes were growing heavy. She nestled against him with another sigh of contentment.

As his hands continued to stroke up and down her back in long, slow comforting movements, she became dimly aware that the relief she felt was gradually turning into something else. The hands on her back were moving in circles now, with a more insistent rhythm, and a slow warmth was building up between them.

Her eyes flew open. She raised her head to look up at him. The sun had set by now, casting the room in dusky shadows. The dark eyes gleamed down at her. Dirk's expression was grave, almost grim.

Their eyes met and held for several long seconds. She stared up at him, mesmerised by the way the dark flecks danced in those deep green pools. She opened her mouth to speak, but no words would come out. Then his head began to bend towards her. She closed her eyes, waiting, longing for his kiss.

When it came, it was exactly as she had dreamed it would be. His mouth was dry and cool, soft, mobile, barely touching hers at first, brushing over her waiting lips like the fluttering wings of a moth. She tightened her hold on his waist, pressing herself up against him, eager for more.

His mouth opened slightly, the pressure became firmer, and the rasp of his beard on her face set her nerve-ends tingling in delicious anticipation. Mindlessly, she parted her lips. Her heart thudded wildly. She was filled with a sense of urgency and need that she had never known before.

Then, with a sudden abrupt jerk of his head, he was gone. His hands moved from her back to her shoulders, gripping them hard, kneading almost painfully, pushing her away from him. In the silence of the room, she could hear the rasp of his laboured breathing as he struggled for control.

She opened her eyes and gazed up at him in confusion. 'Dirk?' she said in a small voice.

But by now he had recovered his composure. He gave her a kind but distant smile and dropped his hands from her shoulders.

'Feeling better?' he asked lightly.

Nicole nodded. 'Yes, I think so.'

Quickly she withdrew her arms from around his waist and ran a hand over her hair, straightening the tangles and tucking the loose wisps behind her ears.

'I have some brandy,' he went on. 'I think we both could use some.'

She nodded again. 'Yes, I think you're right.'

He turned and walked away from her, stopping for a moment to light the hurricane lamp sitting on the table. Then he reached into the cupboard over the counter and took down a bottle and their two tin mugs.

'Nothing very fancy,' he said over his shoulder, 'but it'll have to do.'

She couldn't take her eyes off him. Every movement he made had a new significance to her now. She ached to feel those arms holding her again, those hands stroking her, that mouth on hers.

But it wasn't going to happen, she knew that now. What was more, she had to admit he was right. His unique code of honour wouldn't allow him to take advantage of her vulnerability, her fear, her gratitude, and she loved him all the more for that.

Loved him? She stared at him as he came back across the room towards her. Was this love? She admired him, respected him, longed for his touch. She'd certainly never felt those things for any other man. It was true, then—she was in love with him, probably had been for some time.

'Come on,' he said, 'drink this. You're still in a mild state of shock. Sit down in front of the fire and let me wait on you. I'll get dinner tonight. Then I think a good night's sleep should fix you up.'

'I just might take you up on that,' Nicole said lightly.

She carried her brandy over to the couch and sank down on it. She sat there in front of the fire sipping the fiery liquor while Dirk busied himself lighting the stove and opening cans. In spite of her disappointment that he had felt it necessary to cut short that lovely intimate moment, her heart was singing.

She was in love. For the first time in her life she knew what it meant to want to give herself body and soul to another human being. What was more, whether he knew it or not, she felt certain now that Dirk's feelings for her were far more than the friendship he had once professed.

She gazed into the flames, a secret smile hovering about her lips. At least she knew that he desired her. He'd proved that. And it was a start.

CHAPTER FIVE

IN THE middle of the night, Nicole's deep sleep was shattered by a series of disturbing dreams. Dark threatening shapes loomed up unexpectedly from all sides, finally reaching the terrifying crescendo of a full-blown nightmare.

She was awakened by a loud cry, which she gradually came to realise was her own voice. She was sitting bolt upright in bed, clutching the blanket to her chin and trembling from head to foot.

'Nicole!' came Dirk's voice behind her. 'Nicole, wake up!'

She felt his hand on her shoulder, shaking her, and turned to him. By the light of a pale crescent moon shining in through the window and reflecting brightly on the snow, she could just make out the shadowy outline of his head.

'Oh, Dirk, I'm sorry!' she choked out. 'I'm so ashamed of myself for being such a baby. And for waking you up.' She shook her head to clear the cobwebs. 'I had the most awful nightmare!'

'That's understandable. You had a bad scare today. A nightmare is nature's way of getting all the bogeymen out in the open, of healing. Can I get you something?'

'No, thanks. I'll be all right now.'

Her pounding heart had settled down into its normal rhythm by now, and, as her eyes became more accustomed to the dim light, she saw that Dirk was down on his knees beside the couch, his hair tousled, his chest and shoulders bare.

'Well,' he said, half rising to his feet, 'I'll get back to bed, then.'

'No,' she said quickly, 'please don't go yet.'

'There's really nothing to be frightened of.' There was a hint of impatience in his voice. 'It was only a dream.'

'I'm not frightened,' she said quietly. 'I just want you to stay a while.'

'Nicole,' he said in a warning tone, 'I already told you once...'

'I know what you told me. I'm a big girl. I'll take my chances. I—I just don't want to be alone. Please stay—just for a little while.'

With a heavy sigh of resignation, Dirk rose up all the way, turned around and reached for the poker on the hearth. He stirred up the coals until they glowed hotly, then tossed on a fresh log. It caught immediately, flaring up into a bright tongue of fire.

Nicole drew in her breath as the sudden bright glow outlined the contours of Dirk's form. Although he had on a pair of dark trousers, obviously donned hastily before coming to her, they hung low on his narrow hips, and his bare back and shoulders gleamed in the firelight.

He turned around and stood there for some time with his back to the fire, gazing down at her. She realised then that she herself was far from fully dressed. Since she had Dirk's shirts to wear during the day, she used the long silk blouse she had arrived in as a makeshift nightdress, washing it out each day.

She felt her breath quicken under his steady gaze. Her long dark hair was streaming to her shoulders, and the thin blouse did little to hide the firm slim figure beneath it.

Dirk came back to the couch and sat down beside her. He stared into the fire for a few moments, his features pensive and brooding, then twisted around abruptly to face her. When he spoke at last, his voice was low and throbbing with suppressed emotion.

'This is definitely not a good idea, Nicole.'

'It's not an *idea* at all,' she rejoined quietly. 'There's nothing calculated about it. Neither of us planned it.'

'I'm only a man,' he said in a tight voice. 'Not necessarily the weakest in the world when it comes to women, but I do have my limits.'

'All right, you've warned me. I'm not a child, you know. I'm twenty-five years old, a mature woman.'

His eyes travelled lazily down the front of the thin silk blouse and he nodded appreciatively. 'Yes,' he said, 'you are that. But in spite of your very desirable "maturity", I have the distinct impression you're not as experienced as you like to let on.'

'If you mean I'm not in the habit of hopping into bed with a man on a first date, you're right. I have to care about him before things can get— well, physical between us.'

This was a blatant lie. Nicole had never come close to a full-blown affair. No man had ever awakened the passion in her that slumbered just beneath the cool surface. But she didn't want Dirk to know that, not just yet.

'I see,' he went on. 'And you think you care about me?'

It was a serious question; there wasn't a trace of flippancy in his tone. Still, it gave her pause. He had put her in the position of virtually throwing herself at him, inviting him into her bed, such as it was, and she didn't think she liked that much. She was used to being sought after, not seeking.

There was no way to answer his question, so she remained silent. Then Dirk started speaking again.

'These are unusual circumstances, Nicole. There's no way of knowing how we'd react to each other out in the real world. In fact, two entirely different worlds. Our backgrounds, our lives are diametrically opposed.'

His tone was very reasonable, very convincing, but there was an undercurrent of tension in it he couldn't quite disguise.

'I know all that,' Nicole said quietly.

'I guess what I'm trying to say,' he went on in the same deliberate tone, 'is that I'm damned attracted to you.' He hesitated, then shrugged his shoulders diffidently. 'In fact, if things were different, I could even imagine I might be half in love with you...'

Nicole held her breath. She knew there was a 'but' coming, and waited for it. It didn't matter. He'd already gone further than she'd ever dreamed possible.

When he didn't go on, she couldn't resist a gentle nudge. 'What things?' she asked. 'Are you already involved with someone else?' He'd already told her he wasn't married, quite vehemently, in fact, but there was still that cryptic address book of his.

'No,' came the firm reply. He turned and gave her a direct look. 'I'm not. But you are.'

'Me? But I'm not!'

'What about this guy your father wants you to marry?'

'Victor? I already told you, I have no intention of marrying him. I've never even considered it. That was all my father's idea.' Nicole laughed wryly. 'It's how I got lost in that storm in the first place, running away from my father and Victor.'

Suddenly she'd had enough talk. She'd gone as far as she could with words. If Dirk was that hung up about taking advantage of her, there was no way she could convince him. She'd never thrown herself at a man yet, and she wasn't going to start now.

'All right, Dirk,' she said dully, 'you've made your point. You're probably right.' She forced out a smile. 'Thanks for rescuing me from my nightmare. I'll be all right now.'

'Sure?'

She nodded. 'Quite sure,' she replied stiffly.

Dirk gave her one last curious look, then got up from the couch. He stood there awkwardly for a moment, hesitating, his hands shoved in the back pockets of his trousers, forcing them down even lower so that the thin line of coarse hair that began at his flat abdomen and disappeared beneath the waistband was clearly visible.

Nicole squeezed her eyes shut against the tantalising sight. No more of that! She flopped her head down on the pillow and pulled the blanket up around her shoulders.

After a moment she heard Dirk banking up the fire again, then his slow footsteps as he returned to his own bed. Once again he had withdrawn from her. Nicole could have screamed with exasperation and frustration. She could only lie there, her eyes shut tight, her teeth gritting together.

It was hopeless. There was absolutely nothing more she could do to make this man follow through on the desire they both felt.

Nicole awoke late the next morning. She had slept fitfully, still shaken from the nightmares and still angry, deeply offended actually, at Dirk's pigheaded determination to keep his distance from her.

She heard him stirring in the cabin, all the familiar sounds, filling the bucket with snow, the hiss of the gas flame on the stove as he heated it, the door opening and closing as he went out to the washhouse for his morning bath.

All the while Nicole had kept her eyes firmly closed, her face turned to the fire. She didn't want to see him or speak to him. Next time she heard that helicopter, she vowed silently, she wouldn't waste any time dithering around about whether she wanted to be rescued. She'd run after it until she dropped.

Once she knew Dirk was gone, she opened one eye. The cabin seemed quite dark. Usually Dirk arose at first light. She sat up and peered around. The bright sunshine that ordinarily greeted her in the morning had disappeared.

She got off the couch, slipped on her ski pants and Dirk's red shirt and ran over to the window. The entire sky was filled with a heavy bank of menacing black clouds. It looked very forbidding, even ominous, and she shivered in spite of her warm clothing.

She stood there staring out at the bleak scene for several long minutes. If another storm came up it could be days, weeks, before the helicopter came back. It also meant Dirk wouldn't be able to go off on his daily explorations, and she didn't think she could bear another day, another moment, of the tension between them.

Then, suddenly, she heard Dirk's footsteps just outside the cabin, stamping the snow off his boots. Her whole body went rigid. She didn't want to face him, but there wasn't time to get back to bed. She gripped the edge of the counter and stared stonily through the window. Since there was no way out of it, she'd just have to deal with it as best she could.

In the next moment the door opened, then closed behind him. There was utter silence in the room. Neither of them spoke. Finally, Nicole heard Dirk set the bucket down and take a few steps towards her.

'It looks as though there's another storm brewing,' he said.

'So I see,' she replied curtly.

'I doubt if I'll be able to get any fieldwork done.'

'I guess not.'

There was another long silence. Then he started walking towards her again, each footstep bringing him closer. Nicole closed her eyes, steeling herself against him. Then she felt his presence directly behind her, the tentative touch of his hand on her shoulder. She shrugged it off instantly, twisting away from him, then whirled around to face him with fire in her eyes. Why couldn't he just leave her alone?

'Nicole, is something wrong?' he said in a low voice.

She gave him a falsely sweet smile. 'Why, no,' she drawled, 'of course not. What could possibly be wrong?'

He stared at her for a moment, then shrugged. 'I'd better go get some more wood chopped before it starts snowing.'

She watched him through the window as he went out into the clearing to the pile of logs, glancing up at the sky, which seemed to get blacker by the minute. He moved a log from the pile and placed it on the block, then stood there with his long legs spread wide apart, his arms raised above his head, the axe poised for a second, then swishing down through the air.

With each vicious swing of the axe, she could well imagine that in his mind it was her head lying there on the chopping block, and every graceful, controlled movement he made was another blow to her already breaking heart.

They edged their way around each other in the cabin all that day, barely speaking except for a few brief, very polite necessary requests and replies. Nicole performed her usual tasks, but her heart wasn't in them.

Late that afternoon the first snowflakes began to fall. By evening, the skies had unleashed a full-scale howling blizzard. After their strained and largely silent dinner, Dirk settled himself at his desk to work on his charts. Bored senseless, Nicole got out the greasy playing cards and resumed her games of patience.

At last she heard his chair scrape back. Out of the corner of her eye she saw him get up and stretch, his muscles straining against the woollen shirt. Then he started to prowl restlessly around the room, until he ended up beside the table where she had her cards laid out, and just stood there for a long time looming over her.

She ignored him totally, until suddenly, in one swift movement, he reached down and swept the playing cards to the floor. Nicole gazed up at him in alarm. His jaw was stiffly clenched, his mouth thin and pinched, his expression truculent.

'All right,' he said, 'are you going to tell me what's wrong or am I going to have to beat it out of you?'

What she wanted to do was leap to her feet and slap him—hard. Instead she only muttered, 'If you don't know, there's no point in my telling you.'

Then, without another word, she got down on her hands and knees and started picking up the cards. Dirk stood there for a few moments more, then walked heavily away from her and slammed out of the door.

She finished picking up the cards, turned off the gas lamp, and went over to the couch to make up her bed. She had lost all interest in her card game, and since there was nothing else to do she might as well get in bed. At least if she was unconscious she wouldn't have to think.

She took off her heavy clothes in front of the fire, put on the clean silk shirt she used for a night-dress and crawled wearily into bed. By now Dirk had been gone for quite some time, and as she lay there she couldn't fight down a nagging sense of worry. It beat her where he could possibly be going in that storm. She told herself she didn't even care at that point. If he perished in the snow, she wouldn't shed a tear.

The fire was still burning brightly, and since her couch-bed was directly in front of it most of its warmth fell on her. It wasn't long before she grew drowsy, her eyes became heavy and finally closed. Then, just as she was drifting off, she heard the door open and close. Dirk had come back. That was all right, then.

When she heard him walking towards the couch, her eyes flew open, then closed again. If she pretended she was asleep he wouldn't bother her. She could sense his presence beside the couch, feel the sudden coolness as he stood between her and the fire.

'Nicole,' he said softly.

She didn't answer. Then she sensed that he was kneeling down beside the couch. She felt his hand on her shoulder, and when he spoke again his voice was almost directly in her ear.

'Nicole,' he repeated, more insistently this time.

Finally she opened her eyes a crack, all ready to do battle. But when she saw him, she could only goggle at him, open-mouthed. The heavy black beard was gone! He must have shaved it off just now. In the firelight she could even see a few nicks along his jaw where the razor had scraped too close.

She recognised him, of course, but what a transformation! Although the absence of the beard softened his features, it did nothing to mar his rugged good looks. In fact, he was positively handsome! As she stared at the firm chin, the strong jaw, the sensitive mouth, unable to utter a word, the significance of his action slowly dawned on her.

As she sat bolt upright, Dirk shifted his weight down beside her so that their bodies were touching, and she drew in her breath sharply at the electric shock that ran through her. He had taken off his shirt, leaving his chest and shoulders bare, and the sheer beauty of the man simply took her breath away.

'I want you, Nicole,' he said.

'I know,' she whispered.

'I've tried my damnedest——'

'Shh!' she said, reaching out to place one finger on his mouth. 'Don't talk.'

He grasped her outstretched hand, turned it over and drew the palm up to his lips, lips that burned with the same aching need as her own. Then, with his glittering eyes still boring into hers, he placed his other hand along the side of her jaw. With a gentle but firm pressure, the hand slid slowly downward, over her mouth, her chin, her neck, until it settled on her breast.

The inner tumult created by his touch rocked her beyond belief. Fire coursed through her veins as he moved his hand back and forth over the taut peaks in light, feathery caresses. She felt shaken to her foundations.

Finally, with a low groan deep in his throat, he put his arms around her, crushing her to him. His mouth covered hers in a deep, searing kiss that reached to her very soul. All the pent-up desire of the past month seemed to explode in that one frenzied embrace. Dirk's hands were everywhere now, stroking up and down her back, over her breasts, her stomach, the silky material of her thin shirt sliding sensuously on her bare skin.

He raised his head then and turned her around so that she was lying across his lap, gazing up at him. Slowly he unbuttoned the blouse, spread it apart and stared down at her, his hair falling over his forehead, his breathing ragged.

'So beautiful,' he murmured roughly. 'Just as I knew you'd be.' He put a hand on her breast, moulding its fullness under his fingers. 'So soft, so perfect.'

Nicole twisted towards him so she could touch him, and ran one hand down from his shoulder over his smooth broad chest, his ribcage, his flat abdomen, until it hovered uncertainly at the waistband of the low-slung trousers.

He shuddered, pulling in his breath sharply, then suddenly he clamped his hand over hers, removing it from its dangerous position. Slowly, reluctantly, he pulled the opening of her blouse together, and leaned his head back on the back of the couch.

'Listen,' he said at last. 'Before this gets out of hand, there are a few things we have to talk about.'

Nicole reached up and placed a hand flat on his bare chest. His heart thudded erratically beneath her fingers. When she began to stroke him, he covered her hand with his, stilling it, and she sat up to face him.

'What things?' she asked softly.

'Well, first of all, are you sure you know what you're letting yourself in for?' Dirk asked soberly.

'No,' she replied with a low laugh, 'I don't. But I know what I want, and I've come to know you very well.'

'But that's just it! You don't know me at all. This—whatever you want to call it—this idyll, this adventure we've gotten ourselves into—it can't last. It's not real.'

'The way I feel is real enough,' Nicole protested. She drew back from him and eyed him warily. 'Dirk, are you trying to tell me that you don't care for me?'

His eyes widened incredulously, and he reached out to enfold her in his arms. He pulled her head up against his chest, his chin resting on her hair, his large hands warm and soothing on her back.

'Of course I care about you,' he murmured. 'I told you once I was already half in love with you, and that feeling has only grown. I've never really been in love before.' He laughed. 'Except with my work.'

He loved her! Nicole's heart sang. She nestled closer to him. Dirk loves me! 'Well, then?' she asked. 'And I love you. So what's the problem?'

'It's just that I have serious doubts about how we can ever manage to work things out between us, out in the real world.'

She lifted her head and gave him a long look. 'All I know is that I love you,' she said. 'If we want to be together, somehow it will have to work out.'

His eyes burned fiercely into hers, and his hold on her tightened. 'Heaven help me,' he gritted through his teeth, 'I do love you. And I only hope you're right.'

She grinned at him. 'Then don't you think we've had enough talk?'

For reply, his head came down and he buried his mouth in the hollow of her throat. His hands travelled slowly upward until they settled on her breasts. He left them there for a moment, quite still, weighing them, as though trying to memorise their shape and feel and form.

Then, as he began to stroke her gently, a languorous warmth stole through her, and she could feel her nipples grow taut and hard under the light, feathery touch of his fingers on her bare skin.

She threw her head back, her hair streaming over her shoulders as his lips moved downward into the shadowy valley between her breasts, then closed moistly over one throbbing peak. She moaned deep in her throat at the shock-waves that rocked through her whole body and threw her arms around his neck, plunging her fingers into the crisp dark hair.

Dirk raised his head then and his open mouth came down on hers, drawing her into him, his tongue probing, penetrating. His hands clutched at her hips to press her lower body even more tightly against his powerful arousal.

'Darling,' he choked out, 'I do love you. And I want you so badly.'

'Yes,' she cried. 'Oh, please, yes!'

Gently now, with an obvious effort at control, he shifted his weight so that she was lying flat on the couch while he hovered above her, resting on his elbows. His hair fell over his forehead, his breath came in short, explosive bursts. Slowly, carefully, he buried himself into her to complete their love at last.

* * *

Dirk was gone when she woke up the next morning, a secret smile still hovering about her lips. Although the snow was still coming down in heavy white sheets, she was so intensely happy that they could have been in the midst of a killing tropical hurricane and it wouldn't have mattered to her.

She stretched widely, sleekly, like a contented cat, then jumped out of bed. Dirk had already stirred up the fire and thrown on a fresh log, and the cabin was already so warm that she padded barefoot over to the window wearing only her silk shirt, which was so long anyway that it reached almost to the middle of her thighs. After last night there was no need now for false modesty.

She was just laying bacon in the pan for their breakfast when he came back, carrying a fresh load of wood. Nicole turned eagerly to greet him. He had shaved again, and his face glowed from the cold.

'Good morning,' she said.

As he came towards her, his dark eyes gleaming appreciatively and darting up and down her scantily clad form, she was seized with a sudden attack of shyness. She turned away from him in some confusion and began to poke at the bacon with a fork while he carried the logs over to the fireplace.

When he had set them down and removed his outdoor clothing, he came up to stand directly behind her, so close that she could feel the cold still clinging to him. His arms came around to encircle her midriff, and she drew in a sharp breath.

'Are my hands cold?' he murmured in her ear.

He laid his face next to hers, and she could smell the fresh scent of soap on his skin as it rasped roughly against her cheek. She leaned her body back against his and closed her eyes.

'A little,' she whispered. 'But I don't mind.'

'You know what they say,' he said. '"Cold hands, warm heart."' He nipped at the lobe of her ear.

'Do you have a warm heart, Dirk?' she asked lazily.

'Mmm. For you, I do.' One hand had travelled slowly upward to move across her breast.

'Well, unless you want a burned breakfast,' she said with a laugh, 'you'll have to wait a while before you start to prove it!'

Reluctantly he dropped the hand and went over to sit down at the table. After she dished up their breakfast, Nicole settled herself across from him, basking in his presence, her heart filled with the delights of the night before, the anticipation of things to come.

Dirk ate silently. He seemed distracted, and would glance out of the window occasionally at the snow still coming down, frowning a little, responding to her attempts at conversation in monosyllables, until finally she set her fork down loudly beside her plate to get his attention.

'Dirk,' she said, 'is something wrong?'

He raised his eyes, startled, then gave her a long careful look. 'I've been thinking,' he said heavily, 'that it's probably time for you to leave.'

'What?' She couldn't believe her ears. 'How can you say that now, after—after——?' She broke off.

'You've been here for six weeks,' he went on in the same hard tone. 'No one knows whether you're alive or dead. It's not fair to your father. He should at least know you're all right.'

She could only stare at him, bewildered. 'But how could I? It's not my fault. I admit I was tempted to hide when I heard the helicopter come over, but I didn't, after all. And you can't help it if the radio's broken.'

To her utter amazement, a deep flush began to spread from his neck up over his face. He stared down at his plate, turning his fork over and over on the table. Then he raised his head and gave her a sheepish look.

'Well, the truth of the matter is that the radio isn't broken. I fixed it a week ago.'

Nicole goggled at him. 'You mean to tell me you could have called for them to come and get me?' He nodded. 'A week ago?' she went on. 'That was before this storm came up.' He nodded again.

Suddenly she broke out into gales of helpless laughter. Wiping her eyes, she saw that Dirk was trying hard to look dignified and stern, but that his mouth was twitching.

'You fraud!' she cried at last. 'And all this time I thought you were dying to get rid of me!'

He shrugged. 'Well, I was at first. And the radio really was broken then. In fact, it's not in perfect order now. The batteries are very weak, must have been defective to begin with, and that's why I haven't used it before now, except to test it out once in a while.'

'Before now?' she asked apprehensively, knowing what was coming.

'Yes,' he said flatly. 'Don't you see, darling? It has to be done. As soon as this storm passes over.'

At the look of utter disbelief on her face, he jumped up from his chair and came around to stand

WOW!

THE MOST GENEROUS
FREE OFFER EVER!
From the Harlequin Reader Service®

GET 4 FREE BOOKS WORTH MORE THAN $11.00

Affix peel-off stickers to reply card

FOUR FREE BOOKS 4

4 FOUR FREE BOOKS 4

PLUS A FREE VICTORIAN PICTURE FRAME

AND A FREE MYSTERY GIFT!

NO COST! NO OBLIGATION TO BUY!
NO PURCHASE NECESSARY!

Because you're a reader of Harlequin romances, the publishers would like you to accept four brand-new Harlequin Romance® novels, with their compliments. Accepting this offer places you under no obligation to purchase any books, ever!

ACCEPT FOUR BRAND-NEW

YOURS

We'd like to send you four free Harlequin novels, worth more than $11.00, to introduce you to the benefits of the Harlequin Reader Service®. We hope your free books will convince you to subscribe, but that's up to you. Accepting them places you under no obligation to buy anything, but we hope you'll want to continue with the Reader Service.

So unless we hear from you, once a month, we'll send you 6 additional Harlequin Romance® novels to read and enjoy. If you choose to keep them, you'll pay just $2.49* per volume—a saving of 30¢ each off the cover price, plus only 69¢ for shipping and handling for the entire shipment! There are no hidden extras! And you may cancel at any time, for any reason, just by sending us a note or a shipping statement marked "cancel." You can even return any shipment to us at our expense. Either way, the free books and gifts are yours to keep!

ALSO FREE!
VICTORIAN PICTURE FRAME

This lovely Victorian pewter-finish miniature is perfect for displaying a treasured photograph—and it's yours *absolutely free*—when you accept our no-risk offer.

Perfect for a treasured Photograph

Plus a FREE mystery Gift —follow instruction at right.

*Terms and prices subject to change without notice. © 1990 Harlequin Enterprises Limited. Canadian residents add applicable federal and provincial taxes.

WE EVEN PROVIDE FREE POSTAGE!

It costs you *nothing* to send for your free books — we've paid the postage on the attached reply card. And we'll pick up the postage on your shipment of free books and gifts!

behind her, his hands on her shoulders. He bent his head to hers.

'It's the right thing to do,' he said softly. 'For us as well as your father.'

'I'll never see you again,' she said in a dull, hopeless tone.

'Of course you will.' Dirk crossed his arms over her breasts and kissed her cheek. 'I love you, remember? And in the spring——'

She twisted her head around and gazed up at him, horror-stricken. 'In the spring?' she cried. Then she brightened. 'Why wait so long?' she said eagerly. 'Why not come with me now?'

He straightened up. 'That's not possible, Nicole,' he said in a tight voice. 'I can't leave my work—not yet.' Then his face softened. 'It won't be forever. It's already November. I usually leave the park around the first of March. That's only four months.'

Four months! She didn't think she could bear it. She'd lose him, she knew she would.

'Then let me stay with you,' she pleaded. 'We can call the Forest Service, tell them I'm safe, but that you need me to help you with your work. My father will just have to accept it.'

He walked over to the window and stood there staring out at the falling snow, his hands in his trouser pockets. He didn't say anything for a long time. Finally he turned around, leaned his hips back against the counter and folded his arms across his chest.

'I want you to go, Nicole,' he said quietly. 'We're living in some kind of fairy-tale here, a dream world. It's got to end. I have my work, you have pieces of your own life to pick up. You've seen my world, at least an important part of it. In the spring, I'll see your world. Until then I think we both need some time apart.'

Nicole knew there was no shaking that iron resolve of his. It was that kind of strength that made him Dirk, why she had fallen in love with him. She got up from the table and walked slowly over to him. Slipping her arms around his waist, she pressed her head into his shoulder.

'All right,' she said, 'we'll do it your way.' She raised her face to his. 'But not until the storm is over, right?'

Dirk grinned at her. 'Right.' Then his hold on her tightened, a familiar gleam of desire lit his dark eyes, and he bent down to kiss her softly, his lips lingering on hers. 'But for now,' he murmured against her mouth, 'I've got other things on my mind.'

The storm raged on for two more days, and then it passed as quickly as it had come. When Nicole woke up on that third morning to see a bright shaft of sunshine streaking through the window, her heart sank.

During those two wonderful days, the happiest days of her life, enclosed in the warm cabin with the man she loved, she had had to bite her tongue over and over again to stop herself from begging him once again to let her stay. It would only have spoiled their happiness. She knew him well enough by now to realise that he wouldn't change his mind.

And she had to admit he was probably right. It was just that he had more strength of will than she did. She supposed she should be grateful for that, but watching him now as the sun's rays caught the glints in his dark hair, the broad shoulders and long-muscled arms lying outside the covers while he slept, she couldn't help wishing he shared her weakness.

Under her steady gaze he blinked, then cocked a sleepy eye at her. Immediately he reached out for her and pulled her down in his arms, nuzzling the side of her neck. His hands moved down her back in long, sensuous strokes and he murmured lazy endearments in her ear.

Then he stopped. His hands stilled and he raised himself up on one elbow, staring past her. His body stiffened, and he gazed down at her, his expression grave.

'It's stopped snowing,' he said.

'Yes—I saw.'

He stroked her hair back from her forehead. 'It won't be forever, darling. Only four months.'

Nicole gave him a stern look. 'You'd just better show up at the end of them, *Dr* Morgan, that's all I have to say!'

He grinned lazily. 'Oh, I'll show up, never fear. Now that I've found you, I'll never let you go.'

CHAPTER SIX

NICOLE sat at the dressing-table in her old bedroom staring at her reflection in the mirror. Somehow she kept expecting to look different, that her experience with Dirk at Glacier should have altered her appearance to correspond to the profound change within.

She had been home for two weeks now, and thoughts of Dirk still filled her every waking moment. That last day had been a nightmare—the rescue by helicopter, the flight from Missoula to Los Angeles where her anxiously waiting father met her, the trip by limousine to the big house in Beverly Hills.

Dirk had radioed the ranger station that same day, and throughout the whole painful goodbye while they were waiting for the helicopter later that afternoon Nicole had managed to choke back the tears. It wasn't until they took off and she stared down at the ground where Dirk stood waving at her, growing smaller and smaller, that she finally allowed herself to let go.

She made a face at herself in the mirror. Actually, she did look different. She had kept her hair pulled back in the natural style she had worn at the cabin, her face free of make-up, but here, back in her old setting, what she saw was the face of a stranger.

Culture shock, she thought. She glanced around the beautiful room, her bedroom since childhood, so familiar, yet at the same time so foreign to her now. It was a large room, with deep bay windows overlooking the garden and french doors leading out to a small brick-walled private patio. Before the trip to Montana with her father in September, she had just had it redecorated in shades of soft cool blues and greys to match her own coloring.

Now it was November, and in true Southern California style the sun was shining. Through the open door to the patio she could hear the lawn sprinklers running, the buzzing of bees around the roses, still in full bloom, the low distant hum of a power mower as the gardener trimmed the lush green lawns that surrounded the large impressive house.

It was almost time for lunch. She got up and went to her dressing-room, its long walk-in wardrobe crammed with beautiful and expensive clothes of every description. She chose a sleeveless pale grey linen dress and carried it into the adjoining bathroom.

There on the wide marble counter, beside the vast assortment of lotions and creams, bath oil and make-up, lay Dirk's red shirt, the shirt she had shrunk in her first abortive attempt to launder it. She had worn it on the trip home and wouldn't part with it for the world. It was her only link with Dirk now.

She picked it up and buried her face in it, as though it somehow brought the man himself closer to her.

* * *

There were two guests at lunch that day, Victor Channing and Margot James, Nicole's oldest friend. They ate out on the terrace beside the pool, an enormous striped umbrella shading them from the hot noonday sun.

'I still can't get over it,' Margot was saying between bites of fresh crab salad. 'Lost in the wilderness for weeks, then all of a sudden reappearing. It's like a miracle!'

Margot was as short and round and fair as Nicole was tall and slim and dark. They were as different in temperament as they were in looks, with Margot far more outgoing and vivacious compared to the cooler, more remote Nicole.

Nicole laughed. 'It was a helicopter, Margot. Modern technology, not a miracle.'

Margot wrinkled her snub nose. 'Oh, you know what I mean. Don't be so picky!' She waved her fork in the air. 'What I don't understand is how you can keep so quiet about it. We're all dying to hear all about your hairy adventures, and you don't say a word.'

Nicole felt herself redden. 'Maybe I'm writing my memoirs,' she said lightly, 'and want to save the exciting bits.'

Her father cleared his throat loudly. 'Well, all I know,' he said in a firm authoritative tone, 'is that somehow I intend to reward that young man who rescued you and took you in. He saved your life. What was his name, Nicole?'

'Morgan, Dad,' Nicole murmured. 'Dr Dirk Morgan.'

She loved saying his name, a treat she deliberately denied herself for the most part. At this point

she didn't want to give rise to any suspicions about
the nature of their relationship. It was bad enough
that everyone knew they'd been alone in that cabin
for weeks on end. She didn't want to feed gossip
by discussing Dirk any more than she had to. When
he came for her in the spring and they could de-
clare their love openly, it would be different.

'Right,' her father went on. 'Dr Morgan.' He
turned to Victor Channing. 'From what I hear he's
quite a prominent wildlife biologist. Know anything about him, Victor?'

'Not really,' drawled Victor. 'Nicole will have to
fill us in on the man's finer qualities.'

He had been very quiet all during the meal, but
kept darting covert glances at Nicole, as though
trying to read her mind or trip her up in some way.
Nicole didn't trust him an inch. Although nothing
more had been said about the proposal of marriage
she had so firmly rejected, she knew better than to
believe the subject was closed. Victor was a man
who didn't give up easily.

In his late thirties, with a thin, rather pinched
face and smooth colourless hair, he reminded Nicole
of a sharp-eyed lizard waiting on a rock for its unsuspecting prey. She knew she wasn't being fair. He
had always treated her with elaborate courtesy and
deference, and in his way probably did love her,
just as he loved his extensive art collection and his
beautiful home in Pacific Palisades.

It would be a good marriage too, she realised,
and she didn't blame her father for pressing the
suit. Victor was wealthy, socially prominent, and
one of the most sought-after bachelors in Southern
California. He just didn't appeal to her. He never

had, but especially not now, after having met and fallen in love with Dirk.

Her father wiped his mouth on his napkin, set it beside his plate and glanced at the other man. 'Are you ready to go, Victor?' he asked.

Victor rose slowly to his feet and glanced down at Nicole. 'Will you be coming with us to the opera tonight?'

'Oh, I don't know, Victor. I thought I'd turn in early.' She gave him a deliberately wan smile. 'I'm still a little wobbly.'

'Nonsense,' her father chimed in. 'Do you good to get out, see some of your old friends.'

'I'll see, Father,' she said evenly.

Their eyes locked together for several seconds in a silent contest of wills. Then he nodded curtly and both men turned to go. When they were out of sight, Nicole heaved a deep sigh of relief.

'That bad?' came Margot's amused drawl.

Nicole turned to her with a frown. 'I just wish Father wouldn't keep pushing.'

'Well, he's hardly asked you to run the Boston Marathon,' was the dry reply. 'A night at the opera wouldn't kill you. I mean, you're not injured or suffering from some dread disease you caught out in the wild, are you?'

'Well, no.' Nicole sighed again. 'It's hard to explain. Somehow all this——' She waved a hand in the air to encompass the house, the pool, the grounds. 'It all seems so unreal to me.'

Margot put her elbows on the glass-topped table, leaned forward and gave her a frankly probing look. 'Tell me, Nicole, what really happened out there?'

'What do you mean?'

Margot shrugged. 'Well, I don't know anything about this Dr Morgan, but it seems to me *something* rather significant must have happened between you. You've been like a different person since you've been back.'

'In what way?'

'Well, look at you. I mean, you used to be so perfectly groomed, not a hair out of place, a make-up job a movie star would be proud of, a new outfit on every day.' Margot wrinkled her nose. 'Now you look like—I don't know—some kind of barefoot backwoods maiden.'

Nicole had to laugh. 'Is it that bad?' She drained her glass of iced tea and set it carefully back down on the table. 'It's hard to explain, Margot. I guess I have changed in some ways. Marooned out there in the cabin, I just found out how simple life can really be when all you have on your mind is survival.'

'What's he like?'

'Who, Dirk?'

Margot raised an eyebrow. 'Ah, it's Dirk, is it?'

'Margot, we were alone in the cabin for six weeks. You could hardly expect us to remain on formal terms for long.'

'Well, come on, then, tell me about him.'

Nicole hesitated. She was dying to talk about him to someone, just to make his memory more real, more immediate. Margot was her best friend. She could trust her with at least part of the truth.

'Well, let's see,' she began thoughtfully. 'At first he was terribly rude. You see, the reason he was at Glacier Park in the first place was to work, and the last thing he needed was a helpless klutz like me on his hands. I'm afraid I came on as a pretty spoilt, helpless pain in the you know what.' She smiled reminiscently as she recalled those first days of open warfare. 'Anyway, he made it quite clear right at the beginning that he had no intention of waiting on me or coddling me, and that so long as he was stuck with me I'd darned well better start pulling my own weight.'

Margot wrinkled her nose. 'Sounds charming!'

'But don't you see?' Nicole went on eagerly. 'He was right. Once I got it through my head that I either had to make myself useful or starve—or die of sheer boredom—it was the best thing in the world for me. For the first time in my life I felt—well, needed.'

She went on to relate how she had taken over the household chores, the blunders she had made, how Dirk had taught her to help him in his work, the beauty of the surroundings, the primitive conditions, the episode with the mother bear and her cubs.

'And what does this paragon look like?' Margot asked when she was through.

A mental image of Dirk rose up in Nicole's mind, and she smiled. 'Well, he's tall, well built, and his eyes are a nice deep green with darker flecks in them. He has coal-black hair, very thick and far too long. In fact, he wore a beard when I first met him, but he shaved it off later.' Suddenly realising the implications of that revelation, she went on hastily, 'And he's absolutely devoted to his work with the animals.'

Throughout both these long speeches, Margot's expression had grown more and more thoughtful.

Now she leaned back in her chair and narrowed her eyes at her friend.

'You're in love with him,' she stated flatly.

A hasty denial was already formed on Nicole's lips, when suddenly she wondered why she should bother. She wasn't ashamed of the way she felt. Why not admit it? Margot would keep quiet about it if she asked her to. She could trust her.

But she couldn't do it. It was still too new, too fragile. Talking about it, even to her old friend, might shatter the precious memories. She'd already said too much. Reaching out to place a hand on Margot's arm, she gave her a pleading look.

'Margot,' she said slowly and carefully, 'would you mind terribly if we didn't discuss it any more right now?'

'No, of course I wouldn't mind,' Margot replied hastily.

But Nicole could tell by the hurt look in her eyes that she was offended, and she squeezed the arm affectionately.

'Please try to understand. I'm not being secretive or deliberately hiding anything for no reason. I will tell you one thing. I expect to see him again.'

Margot brightened at that. 'When?'

'He plans to leave the park in early March, so it should be soon after that.'

'And then what?'

Nicole shrugged. 'I'm not sure. We have no definite plans except to see each other in the spring. But, whatever we decide, I promise you'll be the first to know.'

'Well, I guess I'll just have to be satisfied with that, won't I?' Then Margot sat up straight in her chair. 'But what in the world are you going to do about Victor?'

'Nothing,' Nicole replied flatly. 'I turned down his proposal unequivocally before I ever met Dirk Morgan.' She shot her friend a warning look. 'Listen, I don't want either Victor or my father to even consider the possibility that there's a personal relationship between Dirk and me.'

Margot snorted. 'Well, I don't even know that there is one, do I?'

'Please, Margot—trust me. Whatever I've told you, whatever you've guessed, please keep it to yourself. Right now Dirk is Father's fair-haired boy for saving my life. He's even talking about rewarding him in some way. If he finds out there's more to it than that, I'm afraid he—or Victor—would harm Dirk.'

'How could they do that?'

'They're powerful men, Margot, used to getting their own way. Right now Father's in the mood to help Dirk, and until he returns in the spring I don't want to rock the boat.'

'You know you're playing a dangerous game, Nicole,' Margot warned. 'Although I admit I envy you in a way. He must be quite a guy for you to go to such lengths and take such chances to protect him.'

Nicole's eyes shone. 'Oh, he is. You'll see for yourself when you meet him.'

'I can hardly wait.' Margot rose to her feet. 'I have to run now—got a hairdresser's appointment at two o'clock.' She squinted down at Nicole for a moment, then said, 'You know, I really do wish you'd get your hair done or start wearing a little make-up. This is Beverly Hills, you know, not the wilds of the Montana Rockies.'

Nicole ran a hand through her long dark hair. 'Maybe you're right. I'll think about it.'

To please her father, and to keep alive his gratitude and good will towards Dirk, Nicole began gradually to enter into the old social whirl, and as the days passed slowly, with no word from Dirk, the time they had together in the cabin began to take on a fuzzy dreamlike quality.

She would have given anything for some communication from him. She knew it wasn't possible, that the extent of his contact with the outside world was limited to the radio. Still she kept hoping that somehow he would get a message through to her.

With Margot's blunt criticism of her altered appearance still ringing in her ears, she finally did make an appointment with her old hairdresser. Although she firmly insisted on a simpler style than the elaborate creation she used to wear, it still felt like a step backward when she viewed the sleek, polished results.

The new hairstyle seemed to demand the use of make-up, some new clothes, and each small concession to convention only pushed Dirk's memory even farther back in her mind, until finally she began to wonder seriously if it had been all a dream. It seemed so remote now, back in her old home, seeing her old friends, embarked once again on the same old round of parties and luncheons and afternoon bridge games.

She felt as though she were living a double life. When she was with her old friends, she looked, acted and even felt like her old self, but when she was lying in her bed alone at night, her whole body aching for the man she loved, then the images and memories became more vivid, more real, and she would relive every moment of their time together.

She wished she had a picture of him. Only the red shirt, still lying on the counter in her bathroom, convinced her that he really did exist, that they really had fallen in love, and that in the spring he would return. She'd just have to be patient. Dirk had said he'd come for her, and she had to believe he meant it.

It was Christmas Eve. There was to be a party at the tennis club, and to keep the peace Nicole had agreed to go with Victor, but only so long as her father came with them.

Although there had been no more discussion since her return about Victor's proposal of marriage, she knew both men too well to believe they had given up on the idea. They hadn't become rich and powerful through luck. They both knew how to be patient, to wait, to apply pressure at the right time, in order eventually to wear down the opposition.

She was determined this wouldn't happen, that even if Dirk Morgan disappeared out of her life for good she still would never marry Victor Channing.

She had bought a new dress for the occasion, a lovely cherry-red velvet with a close-fitting, scoop-necked bodice held up by tiny spangled straps, and a long full skirt. She was just putting on the diamond earrings her father had given her for

Christmas when the telephone beside her bed began to ring.

When she answered it, all she heard for a few minutes was a crackling on the wire, then, as though from a great distance, the sound of Dirk's voice.

'Nicole?' he said. 'Is that you?'

Her heart simply stopped beating. Her head whirled, and she sank down slowly on the bed to keep from falling. A slow warmth filled her whole body.

'Dirk? Is that you? I can hardly hear you. Where are you?'

'Yes,' he said with a laugh, 'it's me. I'm at the ranger station. I skied down this afternoon just to call and wish you a merry Christmas.'

Tears of joy sprang into her eyes. 'Oh, Dirk, it's so wonderful to hear from you! I miss you so.'

'I know,' he said. 'It won't be long now. Thanks to your efficient help I'm going to finish up earlier than I expected.' He paused for a second, then said, 'Although that's not the only reason. I've got to see you.'

'When?' she asked eagerly.

'I figure I can wind things up here in another few weeks, and, depending on the weather, should be able to leave by the middle of January.'

Nicole was so filled with happiness that she couldn't speak. Dirk was coming in just a few weeks! She'd see him again, hold him in her arms, the real live flesh and blood man. It wasn't a dream. It was the most real thing in her life.

'Nicole?' he was saying in a worried tone. 'Are you still there?'

'Yes,' she said quickly. 'Yes, I'm still here.'

'You haven't changed your mind, have you?' he asked slowly. 'I mean, about us.'

'Oh, no,' she assured him vehemently. 'Far from it. I'm just so excited you're coming sooner than you expected I can't quite take it in. Oh, Dirk, I need you so badly! It's been so empty here without you.'

'Well, that's all right, then,' he said with obvious relief.

There was a loud burst of ominous static, and, although she could still hear his voice faintly, she couldn't make out a word he said. Then the line went dead.

'Dirk?' she shouted into the telephone. 'Are you there?'

But there was no reply, and Nicole slowly hung up the receiver. It didn't matter. He'd said all he needed to. Now she could start counting the days, the hours. She lay back on the pillows, her heart and mind filled with thoughts of Dirk, the sound of his beloved voice still echoing in her mind.

Then, from out in the hallway, she heard her father calling to her. 'Nicole? Victor's here. It's time to go. Are you ready?'

With a sickening lurch in the pit of her stomach, she was yanked back into reality. She sat up on the bed and ran a hand over the back of her hair to straighten it.

'Yes, Father,' she called. 'Give me a few more minutes, and I'll be right down.'

She got up from the bed and went back to her dressing-table to finish putting on the earrings. As she listened to her father's footsteps going away down the hall, she knew that with Dirk's arrival only a few weeks off she would have to tell him the truth about their relationship, and convince him how important it was to her.

Throughout the entire evening Nicole debated ways of tackling the subject to avoid the inevitable conflict. She wasn't looking forward to it. Pleading a headache, she had talked her father into taking her home early. Barely able to be civil to Victor, she hadn't even invited him in when they arrived back at the house, and he had driven off in his dark blue Mercedes with an angry squeal of tyres.

After she had hung up her coat, she went into the library, where her father had settled down in front of the fire to smoke a cigar and have a last glass of brandy.

She rapped lightly on the open door. 'If you have a minute, Father, I'd like to talk to you.'

'Of course,' he replied, half rising to his feet. 'Are you feeling better?'

'Yes,' she replied. She went over to his chair and stood before him. 'It was so noisy and crowded at the club. I guess I'm still having a little trouble getting readjusted.'

'How about a nightcap?'

That sounded like a very good idea. Her nerve needed all the bolstering she could give it. 'Stay where you are,' she said. 'I'll get it.'

She crossed over to the bar that was set against one dark-panelled wall. After pouring out her drink, she walked slowly back to her father and sat down on the couch across from him. She took one quick sip of the fiery brandy, then leaned forward and gave him a long, intense look.

'Father, I had a telephone call this evening before we left for the party. From Dirk Morgan.'

'Oh?'

'He's about to wind up his project in Montana, and plans to come down here on a visit when he's through.'

'Good. I'm very anxious to meet him. I want to thank him personally for all he did for you.'

'He's coming mainly to see me, Father,' Nicole went on slowly.

His eyes narrowed at her. 'I see. And just what does that mean?'

'It means that we—well, we became very good friends during my stay there.'

Her father's face darkened ominously. 'I've always had the feeling you weren't being entirely honest with me about that whole episode. Just what did happen, Nicole?'

'Listen, Father,' she said, annoyed, 'this isn't the Dark Ages, you know. I'm twenty-five years old, after all, a grown woman. Relations between men and women have changed drastically in the past several years.'

'Not for you,' he stated flatly. He got up from his chair and went over to the bar to pour himself another brandy. 'You're not like that. You may think I don't pay any attention to you, but I know you better than you think I do.'

Nicole waited, tense with apprehension, ready to do battle, but when he came back his expression had softened. 'You're very like your mother. Fastidious, I believe, is the proper word.' He shook his head. 'You're no more capable of an indiscriminate affair than she was.'

'Father, I love him,' she said softly, touched in spite of herself at the unexpected tenderness in his voice. 'And he loves me.'

'You sound very sure of yourself. Why haven't you told me this before now?'

'Well, for one thing, I wasn't expecting him back until March, and for another, I knew how set you were on my marrying Victor. I just didn't want to argue about it, and I didn't want to turn you against Dirk before you had a chance to get to know him.'

To her utter amazement, a look of intense pain appeared fleetingly in her father's eyes. 'Is that the kind of father I've been to you, Nicole? That you have to deceive me because you're afraid I'll force you to do something you don't want to do, or seek some kind of revenge on the man you love just because you won't fall in with my plans?'

Nicole leaned towards him and put a hand on his arm. 'Father, I'm sorry if I've misjudged you. But you have to admit you were pretty vehement about my marrying Victor when we first went to Montana.'

'I admit that I had my own reasons—perhaps selfish reasons—for encouraging the marriage, but I also honestly did believe it would have been best for you. No one else seemed to please you, and it was time you settled down.' He covered her hand with his. 'But if you really love this Dr Morgan, and if he loves you, then that's what I want for you.'

'Do you really mean that?' she asked earnestly.

He nodded. 'What's more, I haven't forgotten that he saved your life, and I'm going to find a way to repay him for that. I have some connections in

academic circles, and the company is always looking
for worthwhile causes to invest in for the public
good. Perhaps I can arrange something that will
keep your young man a little closer to home. You'd
like that, wouldn't you?'

'Yes, of course I would.' Nicole rose to her feet
and smoothed down her dress. 'But he's very in-
dependent and strong willed.'

'Well, so am I.'

Nicole had to smile. It would be very interesting
to see these two strong-willed men in action!

She went to bed that night feeling vastly relieved
that it was out in the open now. Her father had
taken it much better than she ever dreamed he
would, and that was some sort of victory in itself.

From then on the days dragged slowly by. Nicole
felt as though she were only going through the mo-
tions of life, held in a sort of suspended animation
where nothing was real to her except the fact that
she'd be seeing Dirk again soon.

Since their fateful discussion on Christmas Eve,
neither she nor her father had mentioned the subject
again. She preferred it that way. She was determined that nothing was going to interfere with
their plans now.

It was already two weeks after Christmas. She
hadn't heard from Dirk again, but he'd said the
middle of January, and that meant only another
week or two before he would be there.

One morning Nicole was in the dining-room
having a late breakfast. The weather had turned
cool and drizzly, as was often the case in Southern
California in January, and she planned to spend

the day at home catching up on her reading. She had just started to leaf through the morning newspaper when she heard the front door open and close and looked up to see her father standing in the doorway.

'What are you doing home?' she asked in some surprise. 'I thought you were chained to that desk of yours all day.'

Without a word, he sat down across from her and poured himself a cup of coffee. Then he reached down into his briefcase on the floor, took out a manila folder and set it on the table.

With no preliminary, he said, 'When do you expect that young man of yours to arrive?'

'Any day now,' she replied, mystified. 'He'd be leaving the park around the middle of January.'

He flipped open the folder. 'I've had one of my men do a little research for me about Dr Morgan.' He turned over some typewritten pages. 'Quite an impressive record. He has a fine reputation in his field. In fact, he's something of a celebrity in certain circles.'

'What's the purpose of all this, Father?' Nicole asked guardedly. She was tense with anticipation. Was there some dreadful secret in Dirk's past she didn't know about? Was her father planning to discredit him publicly just to get her to marry Victor?

'Just how definite are your plans?' he asked, side-stepping her question adroitly.

'What do you mean?'

He shrugged. 'Modern relationships are too complicated for me to fathom. Are you going to marry? Have an affair?'

'Father!' she exclaimed, half amused.

'I'm only asking for information, Nicole,' he said mildly, 'not making any accusations.'

She stared down at her plate, the scrambled eggs and bacon half eaten. What were their plans? They had never really spelled them out. At the time, she had been certain that they were solidly committed to a permanent relationship of some kind, but nothing definite had been settled. There hadn't been time.

She laughed nervously. 'To tell you the truth, we didn't get that far.' She raised her eyes and gave him a defiant look. 'We thought it wiser to get to know each other better in a more normal environment.'

He nodded. 'Very sensible. But how do you feel? Do you want to marry him?'

'Well, yes, as a matter of fact, I do.'

'Then that's all I need to know.'

'Wait a minute, Father. Dirk will have something to say about that, you know.'

He waved a hand dismissively in the air. 'If you want to marry him, he'd be a fool not to go along with it.'

She smiled. 'You're prejudiced!'

'Maybe. At any rate, I see no harm in moving ahead on that basis.'

'Moving ahead? Father, what are you talking about?'

'Here,' he said, handing her the folder, 'take a look.'

Nicole took the folder from him and began to leaf slowly through the typewritten pages until she came to a photograph of Dirk that had been extracted from a popular nature magazine. It had obviously been shot in the desert. He was bearded and unkempt, shaggy-haired, wearing heavy boots and smiling at a very large, very ugly lizard, sunning itself on a nearby rock. She glanced down at the caption.

'Dr Dirk Morgan,' she read silently, 'well-known wildlife biologist, on one of his expeditions in the Sahara to study the indigenous species of native fauna and flora. Dr Morgan is currently dividing his time between conducting graduate seminars at Stanford University in California and field expeditions in various parts of the world.'

'Well?' she said when she was through.

'Well, is that the kind of life you want?' her father asked gravely. 'Wandering around the world at least half the time, unsettled, without a real home, living like gypsies. You haven't been raised to that, Nicole.'

'It's his work!' she exclaimed. 'And his work means everything to him.' She narrowed her eyes to him in a measured, warning look. 'I'm not going to give him up, Father.'

He raised a hand. 'I'm not asking you to. But surely his work doesn't mean more to him than your welfare?'

She sank limply back in her chair and eyed him suspiciously. 'Just what are you driving at?'

'Just this. The company could use a man like this. He's well known, has a worldwide reputation in academic circles. It would be good public relations, improve our corporate image in this ecology-conscious era. And it would mean a settled life for you, in a familiar setting, among your own kind.'

'I don't know,' she said slowly. 'It sounds wonderful, but he's really committed to his work, and has a will of iron. He may not go for it.'

'Well, we can only try. I take it the plan meets with your approval?'

'Oh, yes.' It would solve everything. Their different worlds would come together perfectly.

'Then that's a step in the right direction,' he said with satisfaction.

When the telephone in her bedroom rang early one Sunday morning about a week later, somehow Nicole knew it would be Dirk. She ran to the side of the bed and eagerly snatched up the receiver.

'Hello.'

'Nicole,' came his clear firm voice. 'It's Dirk.'

'Oh, Dirk, it's so good to hear your voice! Where are you?'

'Well, just a few miles away, as a matter of fact.'

'You mean here?' she asked excitedly. 'Here in Beverly Hills?'

'Not quite. I'm at the airport. I flew in from San Francisco early this morning and just got off the plane.'

'Shall I come to pick you up?'

'No. I'm going to rent a car. I just wanted to make sure you were home before I showed up on your doorstep.'

Since she'd been home constantly for the past week, hovering near the telephone waiting for his call, there wasn't much danger of that. After she had given him directions to the house, she dashed around madly trying to decide what to wear. For one brief moment she was tempted to put on the red shirt, still in its place of honour in the bathroom, but at the last minute decided on a simple, beautifully cut pale pink linen dress. Then she ran downstairs to wait for him.

Half an hour later the doorbell rang. Filled with nervous anticipation, she gave herself one last quick glance in the hall mirror and ran to answer it.

CHAPTER SEVEN

FOR a moment they stood there on either side of the doorway simply staring at each other, speechless and immobile.

Dirk looked wonderful—a little rumpled from his plane trip and dressed in a pair of clean, well-fitting blue jeans, a white turtleneck sweater and a dark green corduroy jacket with leather patches on the elbows. His crisp shiny black hair had recently been cut, still a little on the long side, and he was clean-shaven.

'Well,' he said at last. 'Aren't you going to invite me in?'

'Oh, I'm sorry,' Nicole cried. 'I'm just so glad to see you I've forgotten my manners.' She opened the door wider. 'Please come in.'

When he had stepped inside, she closed the door behind him and leaned up against it, watching him, basking in his presence. He stood in the large, tile-floored entrance hall gazing around at the fine Queen Anne table against one panelled wall, the ornate gilt mirror hanging over it, the wide sweep of the staircase, the fine paintings on the wall.

He gave her a quizzical look. 'Quite impressive. A far cry from the cabin.'

She laughed nervously. This wasn't going at all as she had anticipated. Why did he seem so remote and aloof, even critical of the lovely home she had simply taken for granted all her life? Why didn't he just take her in his arms and kiss her? He hadn't even touched her.

She moved a step closer to him. 'You look wonderful, Dirk.'

He gave her a sweeping glance, from her head down to her toes. 'So do you,' he said. 'Different, but as beautiful as ever.'

'How do you mean, different?' she asked warily.

He shrugged. 'I'm not sure. You look so—so polished, so perfect. Nothing like the bedraggled waif I found on my doorstep last fall. In fact, I would hardly have recognised you.'

Her face fell under his silent scrutiny. 'Dirk, are you disappointed?'

'No,' he reassured her hastily, 'of course not. I guess I'm just wondering which is the real Nicole West.'

'Believe me, I'm exactly the same person,' she said earnestly. 'Nothing has changed.'

'Are you sure?'

'Absolutely.'

Then at last he reached out for her. 'Then why don't you prove it to me?' he murmured.

She moved eagerly into his warm embrace. Safe in his arms, she nestled up against him with a sigh of contentment. They stood there quite still for several long moments, enjoying the feel of each other. Finally she raised her face to his.

His hold on her tightened, his head came down and his mouth met hers, warm and reassuring, just as she remembered. Yet she still sensed a reserve in him, a holding back, and he broke off the kiss before it deepened.

Disappointed, even a little hurt, Nicole fought off the nagging doubts, the fear that threatened to rise up out of control and spoil everything. This sense of strangeness would pass, she was certain of it. It would just take a little time.

'How long can you stay?' she asked.

'About a week.'

'And then what?'

'I haven't decided yet. I could take on a graduate seminar at the university for the spring quarter, but the foundation that gave me the grant for the Glacier Park project wants me to go back there next month to finish it up.'

'But I thought you already had finished.'

Dirk shook his head and gave her a wry smile. 'That was just smoke.' The green eyes gleamed, the dark flecks dancing. 'I cut it short to come and see you.'

Reassured by this open declaration, Nicole debated telling him about her father's plan to find a job for him in his company as another possible alternative for his future. But before she could make up her mind she heard footsteps behind them, her father's stertorous throat-clearing, and she hastily broke out of Dirk's loose embrace.

'Father,' she said, turning to him, 'this is Dirk Morgan. Dirk, my father, Marshall West.'

As the two men shook hands, Nicole watched them nervously. Although they greeted each other cordially enough, somehow she was reminded of two male panthers, circling each other warily, sizing each other up, each ready to defend his own territory.

'I can't tell you how glad I am to meet you at last,' her father was saying heartily. 'And to thank you personally for saving my daughter's life.'

'Not at all,' Dirk replied with a diffident nod. 'There were no heroics about it. As a matter of fact,' he went on, giving Nicole a fond glance, 'she became quite a help to me in my work.'

'Ah, yes,' the older man said. 'Your work. Quite an impressive reputation you've built for yourself. I've been reading up on your exploits, you see.'

Dirk only nodded. Nicole, sensing danger, went up to him and took his arm.

'Would you like some coffee?' she asked. 'Or how about some breakfast?'

'No, thanks. I ate on the plane.' He glanced at his watch. 'I really should be on my way now, as a matter of fact. I have a reservation at the Beverly Wilshire Hotel and still have to check in and get settled.'

'Nonsense!' Marshall West boomed. 'You'll stay with us, of course. We have plenty of extra bedrooms.' He glanced at Nicole.

'Yes, Dirk,' she said, 'please do. I've been planning on your staying here.'

Dirk hesitated, frowning slightly, and Nicole could sense his resistance to the idea. She wished she had been the first to suggest it. As usual, her father was coming on too strong, directing the household operations the same way he did his business affairs.

'Father,' she put in hurriedly, 'if Dirk would feel more comfortable in a hotel, then that's up to him.'

When he opened his mouth to protest, she shot him a warning look, and he grimly clamped it shut again. 'Well, of course,' he said grudgingly. 'Whichever he prefers——'

'I'll be delighted to stay here,' Dirk broke in firmly. 'I just don't want to put you to any trouble.'

'Well, that's settled, then,' Nicole said with relief, and, before her father could say another word, she began leading Dirk to the stairway. 'Come on,' she said, 'I'll show you to your room. You can get your bags later.'

They went up the wide carpeted stairs to the second floor landing and walked down the hall until they came to the bedroom she had prepared for him weeks ago, right after his call at Christmas telling her he was coming.

Once inside, she went over to the windows and drew the curtains, letting in the morning sunshine. 'I think you'll be comfortable in here,' she said. 'You have your own bathroom and plenty of closet space. My room is just——'

'Nicole!' he broke in abruptly.

Startled by the urgency in his voice, she turned around to face him. 'Yes?'

'Come here,' he said in a softer tone.

She walked slowly back to him, and when she stood before him he placed his hands on her shoulders and gave her a long, searching look.

'It'll be all right,' he said in a low voice. 'Quit worrying. We only need a little time to get reacquainted. Just relax and let it happen naturally.' He hesitated, then tightened his hold on her shoulders. 'My feelings for you haven't changed.'

She put her arms around his waist and leaned up against him. 'Nor mine for you.' She looked up at him. 'I've missed you so much,' she whispered.

His mouth came down on hers then in a long, tender kiss. She could sense the desire in him by the way his hands moved possessively over her back, the way the mobile mouth pulled at hers. But it was a passion held rigidly in check, and in just a few moments he lifted his head and dropped his hands at his sides.

'I'm dying for a shower and a shave,' he said, smiling and rubbing a hand over his stubbly jaw. 'Think I'll get my bags now and get settled in.'

It would be all right, she told herself as she set the table for lunch. She wished they could have been alone at their first meeting, that he'd come any day but a Sunday, when her father rarely left the house. It was so awkward having him breathing down their necks.

When she was through, she glanced over the table. Did it look too formal? She had used her mother's best Royal Doulton china, the most fragile crystal, the heavy sterling silver. A low bowl of early tulips was set in the middle. No, she decided, Dirk was the kind of confident, self-assured man who would be at home in any situation. There was no need to change her usual habits for his sake.

He should be finished showering by now, and she went upstairs to tell him lunch would be ready in half an hour. At his door, she rapped lightly. When there was no answer, she opened it and poked her head inside.

There was still a light haze of steam wafting from the bath, the scent of very masculine soap, and she could hear the buzz of an electric razor. These sensual reminders of his presence in her house brought back all the memories of their time together in the cabin, and she was suddenly filled with the same old longing for him.

She debated for one brief moment, then shut the door quietly and walked swiftly over to the open bathroom door. She stopped short when she caught sight of Dirk's reflection in the mirror.

He was standing there shaving, leaning forward slightly over the counter to get a closer look in the mirror. She drew in her breath sharply. He was naked except for the towel that was tucked loosely around his lean hips, and there were still drops of water on his broad back and glistening on his hair.

Suddenly he raised his eyes and met her glance. Without a word, Nicole stepped inside, took another towel off the rack and began to slowly wipe the moisture from his back. When she was through, she slipped her arms around his motionless form and pressed herself up against him.

She heard the quick intake of breath, felt the muscles of his chest quiver under her touch. Then he switched off the razor, set it down on the counter and turned around to face her.

'This won't do, Nicole,' he said, gently removing her hands.

'What do you mean?'

The green eyes burned into hers. 'I want you,' he ground out between clenched teeth. 'Heaven knows, I want you. But not here—not in your father's house, under his nose. I couldn't do that.'

'Why, Dirk!' she cried, astonished. 'You prude! I had no idea you were so old-fashioned.'

He shrugged, reddening slightly. 'Call it what you will.' His eyes narrowed at her, glistening. 'What I want to do is unbutton that fetching pink dress of yours, tear it off and make mad, passionate love to you. And I will, believe me. It's all I've thought of for the past two months. But not here.'

He meant it, she had no doubt about that. And if he could restrain the desire he so obviously felt for the sake of a principle, then so could she.

'Well, in that case,' she said lightly, 'I'm sorry I didn't let you go to the hotel.'

'I still can,' he responded immediately. 'It was your choice, remember?'

'All right,' she said, drawing away from him with a sigh. 'Have it your way.' She cocked her head and gave him a wicked grin. 'But you look very tempting in that little towel.'

Dirk raised his arm and pointed at the door. 'Out!' he commanded sternly.

'Yes, sir!' she rejoined smartly. With a little mock salute, she turned from him and left.

The three of them ate lunch together in the dining-room. Since anything could happen if these two strong-minded men locked horns, Nicole viewed the prospect with some apprehension. However, the meal passed pleasantly and without any overt hostility.

Although she kept waiting for her father to raise the subject of Dirk's coming to work for him, he didn't even mention it once. She tensed up every time the issue was skirted, but by the end of the meal Dirk seemed relaxed and unsuspecting. Once again, she thought wryly, her father's delaying tactics had paid off.

They chatted amiably, mostly about Dirk's work, about which Marshall West seemed to have an abundance of information. Dirk was clearly impressed at this display of knowledge, and, by the time coffee was served, had warmed eagerly to the subject.

Then, out of the blue, the older man abruptly changed the course of the conversation. He lit a fragrant cigar, leaned back in his chair with a sigh of contentment and fixed Dirk a suspiciously benevolent look.

'Tell me about your family, Dirk,' he said mildly.

Dirk darted one brief inscrutable look at Nicole, then his face seemed to close up entirely. Slowly and deliberately, he reached into his jacket pocket and took out a packet of cigarettes. After lighting one, he turned back to his host.

'Actually, I don't have any,' he said tersely. 'My parents were both killed in an automobile crash my first year in college. I was an only child, with no other relatives that I know of.'

Nicole stared at him, torn between pity for his loss and annoyance that he had never told her that before. Dirk didn't even glance her way.

'They must have left you comfortably fixed,' her father probed. 'You were able to go on to what must have been several years of expensive education.'

'Not really,' Dirk replied. He seemed more at ease now that the painful subject was out in the open, but his tone was still guarded. 'I was lucky. I managed to scrape by on research assistant jobs and scholarships.'

'Very commendable,' said Marshall West with an approving nod. 'But I'm curious. With your background and reputation, I'm certain you could command high fees in the private sector just on the basis of your name, especially with ecological issues so prominent these days. Surely the work you do can't be very profitable?'

'No,' Dirk replied, 'it's not. But I get by. And it's the work I've chosen, the work I love, am good at.' He hesitated and ground out the half-smoked cigarette. 'Actually, I'm negotiating now with a publisher on a book contract that promises to be rather lucrative, if the advance they're offering is any indication.'

Another surprise! Nicole opened her mouth to ask him why he'd never told her he was writing a book, then snapped it shut again. Now wasn't the time to get involved in that kind of discussion.

She got up abruptly from her chair. 'I thought I'd take Dirk for a drive, show him some of the sights.'

'Oh?' her father said. He turned to Dirk. 'Then you're a stranger to the Los Angeles area.'

'No,' said Dirk, rising to his feet, 'I'm not. As a matter of fact, one of the reasons I came down here was to talk to some people—at UCLA, USC, Occidental—about funding my next grant.' He smiled at Nicole. 'Not, however, the main reason.'

As they walked out to Dirk's rental car, parked in the wide circular drive in front of the house, Nicole moved stiffly ahead of him, seething with suppressed indignation at all the secrets he had kept from her, and the minute they were inside the car she turned on him with fire in her eyes.

'Dirk, why didn't you tell me about the book contract?' Before he could reply, she rushed on. 'Or that you came to Southern California on business? Or about your parents?'

'Hey!' he exclaimed, raising a hand to ward off the barrage of questions. 'Hold on a second! I didn't tell you because those things didn't seem important. What difference does it make that I have no family, or am writing a book?' He reached out and took her hand in his. 'And the talks at the schools are only side issues. I came down here to be with you.'

Nicole's gaze faltered. She still wasn't entirely reassured, but she had to admit that the things that had always seemed so important in her world— family, professional advancement, money—held only a minor place in Dirk's. She'd always known that. Why should it bother her so much now?'

He put an arm around her and drew her closer up against him. 'Those things don't matter,' he said softly. He buried his face in her hair, then raised his head and swore softly. 'Damn! What's wrong with your hair? It's as stiff as a board.'

She laughed. 'It's only hair-spray. It keeps it in place. Remember, I had to do without such niceties at the cabin.'

He removed his arm from her shoulder and started the car. 'Well, I prefer it the way it was.'

Nicole was about to retort that maybe she preferred not to be kept in ignorance about his plans, his background, but stopped herself in time. How in the world did they get off on such a rocky start? From now on, she vowed silently, she'd make more of an effort to understand his point of view, to please him, and she'd start by washing out the hairspray as soon as they got back.

As Dirk made off down the driveway, she moved closer to him and put a hand on his knee. He smiled at her and covered the hand with his.

'Where to?' he asked. 'Some place where I can kiss you, I hope.'

After the tensions of those first few hours together, the days passed quickly for Nicole in a pleasant haze of pure happiness. She loved having Dirk in the house, even though he stuck to his guns about not making love to her under her father's nose.

She grew more certain of her love for him every day, and more secure in Dirk's love for her. By tacit agreement they used this time to become better acquainted and avoided making any definite plans for the future, but each day she became more convinced that it would have to be together.

As far as she knew, her father hadn't yet raised the issue of the job he had in mind for Dirk. He seemed to understand without being told that they needed this time to get to know each other better. Nor were there any more inquisitions about his background after that first tense luncheon.

As they spent more time together, the initial strangeness between them gradually wore off. Nicole was anxious to show him her world, but so far had avoided introducing him to any of her friends. Not only did she think it best to ease gradually into including him in her old life, but most of all she wanted him all to herself for as long as possible.

Dirk spent most mornings conferring with the university people on his agenda, then in the afternoons and evenings they explored the area's points of interest—old Olvera Street with its colourful Mexican booths, an open-air pop concert at the Hollywood Bowl, a trip down to San Diego to visit the famous zoo.

On Thursday afternoon, they took a drive east through Orange County, with its mile after mile of citrus groves, and ended up at Newport Beach, virtually deserted at this time of the year except for the local inhabitants.

'I can see why the beach is so empty,' Dirk commented, as they strolled hand in hand along the wide sandy shore. He stopped to zip up his dark green wind-breaker against the strong breeze blowing off the ocean.

'You should be here at Easter,' said Nicole with a laugh. 'It's wall-to-wall bodies during spring break. High school and college students congregate from all over Southern California. It's an old tradition.'

'Something like Santa Cruz up north. That was our hang-out.'

'I wish I'd known you then,' she said, gazing up at him. He stood straight and tall, his dark hair blowing in the wind. 'I'll bet you were one of those long-haired and bearded hippie protesters.'

Dirk threw back his head and laughed. 'Hardly. My father was a small-town doctor, a pillar of conservatism. He made it very clear that I could either conform or get out and shift for myself.'

'I'd hardly call you a conformist now.'

He shrugged. 'Dad was strict, but, so long as I kept to a few ironclad rules, he left me pretty free to pursue my own interests.'

'It sounds as though you were very close to him,' she said softly. 'It must have been hard to lose him.'

'I guess we were close in a way. I admired him and looked up to him. But it was my mother who really encouraged my enthusiasm for wildlife.' He laughed. 'She had to put up with a wide assortment of it while I was growing up—lizards, snakes, frogs, you name it! Anything that moved, I collected.'

'I never knew my mother,' Nicole said sadly. 'She died when I was born.'

He gathered her into his arms and held her silently for a long time. She felt so safe with him, so at home. If only he would stay here and take the job with her father, it would be perfect.

She only hoped her father would approach Dirk tactfully. It would solve everything if Dirk would agree, but she was afraid it wouldn't be easy to convince him of that. She hadn't mentioned the subject herself. She wanted to wait to see what his reaction to the proposal was first. For all she knew, he might jump at the chance; most men would. But then Dirk Morgan wasn't most men.

The week passed so swiftly that before she realised it it was Saturday already. There was to be a party that night at the Malibu Beach home of one of her father's business associates to which they were all invited. That morning Nicole and Dirk were sitting out on the terrace discussing it over a late breakfast.

'I'm afraid it will be formal,' Nicole said dubiously. 'Will that be a problem for you?'

Dirk gave her a look of amusement. 'I'm not a total hick,' he said mildly. 'Black tie or white?'

'I don't think it matters,' she murmured, abashed. 'We don't even have to go if you don't want to.' She sighed. 'It's hard to believe the week is over and you'll be leaving tomorrow. I've loved having you here, Dirk. Can't you stay a while longer?'

'Afraid not. I still haven't made up my mind whether to take the teaching post at Stanford this spring, and I have an appointment on Monday to discuss it with the faculty head.' He hesitated a moment, then took her hand in his. 'Come with me, Nicole,' he said.

She widened her eyes at him. 'To Stanford?'

'No. To my place in San Francisco.' The green eyes glistened and his hold on her hand tightened. 'It's been hell this past week keeping my hands off you. I want us to be together, really together, for a while. And I think before we make any definite plans you should see something of my world.' He laughed. 'It's not entirely restricted to mountain cabins, you know. I have a life, friends, and I'd like to show you off to them.'

She thought quickly. 'Yes,' she said, 'I'd like to come with you.'

'Will your father get out his shot-gun?'

'Hardly. He may not like it much, but if he thinks——' She stopped short, reddening.

'What?' he prompted. 'If he thinks I'm going to make an honest woman of you eventually?'

'Something like that,' she said with a smile.

Dirk put a hand on her face and kissed her lightly. 'It's what I want, Nicole. I do love you.' He stroked her hair back from her forehead, hair that hung loosely to her shoulders now, clean and fragrant. 'But there are hurdles. I always told myself that when I married it would be forever. It's why I've delayed so long. I never met a woman I thought I could make a permanent commitment to. Until I found you wandering around in the snow.'

'I love you too, Dirk,' she said softly. 'And I know we can work things out.'

'Then you'll come with me tomorrow?'

'Yes, I'll come with you. Anywhere you say.'

The beach house was lit up magnificently, the driveway lined with expensive automobiles. When Dirk had shown up earlier, dazzling in his black dinner-jacket, Nicole had to wonder why she'd ever worried that he wouldn't fit in her world. He would be at home on the moon!

She had worn the red velvet dress she'd bought at Christmas, and when she saw the appreciative look in his eye, aflame with the light of desire, she knew she'd made the right decision to go to San Francisco with him tomorrow.

When she had made the announcement to her father that afternoon, all primed to do battle with him over it, he'd simply nodded and said she was an adult and had the right to conduct her life any way she pleased, that he liked Dirk and trusted her good sense.

To her knowledge, he still hadn't broached the subject of the job to him. If she knew her father, he certainly hadn't dropped the idea, and his ready acceptance of her trip to San Francisco only confirmed her feeling that, in Marshall West's mind, it was a foregone conclusion that they would marry and that Dirk would be absorbed into the family business. She only hoped he was right.

Their host for the party was Douglas Campbell, executive vice-president of the company, and, as they made their way down the stairs from the parking area into the already crowded room, he came forward immediately to greet them, just as though he'd been waiting for them.

He was a short, heavy-set, balding man, whose rather cuddly appearance and avuncular manner were belied by the hard pale blue eyes that glittered behind his black-rimmed glasses.

'Marshall,' he said, 'good to see you. Nicole, you're looking as beautiful as ever.' He turned his gaze on Dirk. 'And this must be our celebrity.' He stuck out a hand. 'Douglas Campbell,' he said.

While the three men chatted, Nicole glanced around the enormous living-room. There was a large buffet table, a bar, and at one end of the room a small orchestra was playing old show tunes. One wall was made entirely of glass, overlooking the beach several feet below, and out on the wide deck a few couples were dancing.

She saw several people she knew, including Victor Channing and Margot, who were sitting together on a couch in one corner of the room. When Margot noticed Nicole, she raised a hand, then said something to Victor. They both got up and came walking towards the little group still standing at the entrance.

When they arrived, Nicole introduced them to Dirk, and after a few moments of idle conversation there was a slight pause. In the next moment, Douglas Campbell exchanged a look with Nicole's father, who gave him an imperceptible nod.

'What say we adjourn to the study,' said Douglas in a deceptively casual tone. 'Dirk, will you join us?'

Nicole was instantly on guard. She looked at Dirk, trying to catch his eye, all ready to come to his rescue at the least sign of distress. But if any man ever looked less in need of rescuing, it was Dirk Morgan.

It helped, of course, that he towered over the other three men and looked like a fashion plate in his perfectly tailored evening clothes. Captains of industry they might be, but, from the rather amused half-smile on Dirk's face and the firm set to his jaw, Nicole knew that he was more than a match for them, singly or all together.

He merely nodded at Douglas, and the four men turned and made their way through the crowd. Nicole watched them every step of the way, still vaguely apprehensive. She had no doubt this casual retreat had been orchestrated by her father, and she prayed he would be tactful—and successful.

'Well!' she heard Margot say at her side. 'So that's the man you were marooned with for six weeks!'

Nicole turned to her. 'Yes, that's the man.'

'Lucky you,' Margot murmured with feeling. 'He's a dreamboat!'

Nicole laughed. 'I don't know if he'd appreciate that description! But I have to agree with you. Listen, I could use a drink.'

They walked together over to the bar, and, after being served with glasses of champagne, strolled out on to the wide deck. It was a bright starlit night, quite balmy for January, and they stood at the railing gazing out at the pounding phosphorescent surf.

'So,' said Margot. 'What are your plans?'

Nicole took a sip of champagne, then said slowly, 'Nothing definite yet, but it looks promising.' She paused for a moment, then decided there was no point in trying to hide anything from her friend. 'Actually, I'm going with him when he leaves tomorrow. He has an apartment in San Francisco.'

Margot's eyes flew open. 'You mean you're going to elope?'

'No. As I said, we haven't made any definite plans. We both think we need to get to know each other better first. We come from such different worlds. He's had a taste of mine this past week, now I want to see more of his than that mountain cabin.'

Margot shook her head wonderingly from side to side. 'I never thought I'd see the day,' she said drily. 'Nicole West, so smitten with a man she'll run off with him without a ring on her finger! I can't say I blame you. If he's half as nice as he is good-looking, I'd say you have a real prize.'

'Well, nice isn't quite the word I'd use,' said Nicole with a smile. 'But he's a real person, with genuine convictions and a brand of integrity you don't see often these days.'

'Plus the fact that he's quite a hunk.'

Nicole laughed. 'Well, yes, there is that.'

Margot launched into a long description of a new hairstyle she was thinking of trying, and as she chattered on Nicole only listened with half an ear. She kept trying to visualise the scene between the four men in Douglas Campbell's library, wondering how Dirk was taking their proposal, hoping he wouldn't just reject it out of hand.

Finally she couldn't stand the suspense another second. Margot had run down by now and was giving her curious looks. Nicole shivered a little.

'It's getting a little chilly,' she said. 'Let's go back inside.'

Back in the living-room, the men had already returned and were standing at the bar. One glance at the set look on her father's face told Nicole that something had gone wrong. Quickly she hurried over to Dirk's side.

'Ah, there you are,' he said with a smile.

She put her arm through his. 'How about dancing with me?'

'I think I can manage that.'

He tilted his head back and drained his half-finished drink, and they went back out on to the deck, deserted now that the evening had grown so cool. When his arms came around her, holding her close, she leaned up against him and twined her arms loosely around his neck, feeling warm and safe in his strong embrace.

They danced in silence for a while to a slow tune coming from inside. Nicole waited patiently, but, when Dirk made no mention of what had happened in the library, finally she had to ask. She drew back a little and looked up to examine his face.

'Well, how did it go in there?' she asked lightly.

He laughed and tightened his hold on her. 'Fine, from my point of view. I'm not so sure about the others.'

'What do you mean?'

He shrugged. 'It's quite simple. They offered me a job and I turned it down.'

She froze. 'Just like that?'

'That's right.'

'But why?'

He raised his eyebrows. 'Why? Because I don't want to spend my life sitting at a desk in some stuffy corporation that makes plastics, or whatever it is. That's not my idea of a satisfying career. Anyway, I already have a job.'

'But I was hoping you'd at least consider it.'

Dirk stopped dead on the dance-floor and frowned down at her. 'Then you knew about it,' he stated flatly.

'Well, yes, in a way. I know how grateful Father was to you for saving my life. This is his way of showing it.' This wasn't going at all as she'd hoped, and she was beginning to grow annoyed at his stubborn attitude. 'I don't see what's so terrible about it. I mean, jobs like that don't come along every day of the week. It would give you a secure position with a great future, and besides, it would solve everything for us.'

'I think what you really mean,' he said in a careful measured tone, 'is that it would solve everything for you and your father.' When she didn't say anything, he shook his head. 'I had no idea it was so important to you.'

He seemed to be slipping away from her, and, panic-stricken by now, Nicole reached out for him. 'Dirk, nothing is more important to me than you, than our love, our future together. I just want you to be fair and not turn down an opportunity like this without even thinking it over. That's all I ask.'

He gazed off over her head into the distance, still frowning. 'All right,' he said at last. 'Maybe you're right. I'll ask your father to give me some time to think it over.' He drew her into his arms again. 'And you are coming with me tomorrow, aren't you?'

'Oh, yes,' she said. She leaned up against him, weak with relief. ''That's all settled.'

CHAPTER EIGHT

EARLY the next morning they started out on the drive north up the coast to San Francisco. Although it was much cooler on the high cliff road that wound past the ocean, especially as they went further north, it was another bright sunny day, with a sparkling blue sky reflected in a calm sea.

They'd been travelling about an hour, and, although so far neither had mentioned the burning subject of the job, it was still uppermost in Nicole's mind, especially after the conversation she had had with her father that morning, which still haunted her.

She had been all packed, ready to go. Dirk had gone out right after breakfast to get the car serviced for the trip before they left, and she had just carried her bags down to the entrance hall to wait for him when her father appeared at the top of the stairs. A late riser on Sunday, he was still in his dressing-gown and slippers.

He came slowly down the stairs until he stood before her. 'I see you're all ready to leave,' he said, glancing at her luggage.

'Yes. Dirk just went to check the car out.'

'I suppose you already know he turned our offer down flat last night?'

Nicole nodded. 'He told me. But, he did say he was going to think it over,' she added hastily.

'Yes, and I agreed to give him ample time to do so. But I also warned him that I couldn't keep the offer open indefinitely. I have Douglas and Victor to contend with, their interest to consider. Do you think he'll change his mind?'

'I don't know,' she replied. 'He's pretty strong willed.'

'Surely you have some influence on him?'

Nicole laughed wryly. 'I wouldn't be too sure about that, not where his work is concerned.'

Her father gave her a long searching look. 'What do you want, Nicole?' he asked quietly.

'I want Dirk to be happy, of course. His work is important to him. I can't ask him to give it up just to please me.'

'You haven't answered my question. What do *you* want?'

She shook her head. 'I'm just so confused. I don't know what I want. It would be wonderful if he'd take the job, settle down here. Otherwise...'

She didn't dare think of what the alternative might be. In the two months she'd been home she had slipped so naturally, so easily, into the familiar pattern of her comfortable life. Could she give that up now? And for what? They'd never even discussed that.

As if echoing her thoughts, he said, 'Have you considered what it will mean if you have to adapt yourself to his way of life permanently?'

Nicole looked down at her feet, unable to meet her father's eyes, and remained silent, as his voice went on, calmly, reasonably, inexorably, driving each point home with inescapable clarity.

'You would have to give up your pleasant home, your friends, your security, your whole way of life, your very identity, to follow this man heaven knows where, while he makes no concessions whatsoever.'

She raised her head and gave him a stricken look. 'Don't you think I know that?' she cried. 'Father, I love him! What am I supposed to do?'

'You can use whatever influence you do have on him to get him to change his mind,' he said flatly. Then his tone softened. 'I'm only thinking of you, Nicole. I want you to be happy.'

'I know,' she said with a sigh.

He patted her awkwardly on the shoulder in an unaccustomed gesture of affection. 'You're a sensible girl. You'll find a way. At least you can try to talk some sense into him.' He paused. 'And if it doesn't work out, Victor will still be there.'

She was just about to retort that, no matter what happened between her and Dirk, she'd rather stay single the rest of her life than marry Victor, when a car door slammed out in front.

'Here he comes now,' she said. 'It's time to go.'

Looking at Dirk now, his hands resting easily on the steering-wheel, his dark hair blowing in the breeze coming in through the open window, Nicole wondered if she should try again. They had passed through Santa Barbara and were on the outskirts of San Luis Obispo when they came across an orange-juice stand at the side of the road.

'How about a glass of juice?' asked Dirk.

'Sounds good.'

He pulled up under the shade of an enormous pepper tree, and while he went over to the stand

Nicole got out of the car to stretch her legs. When he came back with two paper cups full of foaming freshly squeezed juice, they sat down on a bench under the tree to drink it.

It was very peaceful and quiet on the sparsely travelled road. Most of the north-south traffic was jammed on to the interstate that traversed the San Joaquin Valley, leaving the winding, slower coast road virtually deserted. Nicole looked over at Dirk, and took a deep breath.

'Dirk,' she said, 'about the job...'

'Not now, Nicole,' he said softly, meeting her gaze. 'Please. I spoke to your father later last night at the party, and he agreed to give me a week to think it over. I want to be fair, to you and to him, but please, give me a little room. Let's just enjoy the time we have together now, then at the end of the week we'll talk about it and make our decision.'

'All right,' she said reluctantly.

At least he was thinking of it as 'our' decision, and that was some comfort to her. Whatever he had in mind, apparently it was going to include her wishes, and for now she would have to be satisfied with that.

Dirk's apartment was a revelation to her, not at all what she had expected. Set high on Telegraph Hill, it overlooked the city, with a panoramic view of the Golden Gate and the bridge that spanned the bay. It was a very masculine room they entered, large and roomy, with comfortable chairs, a stone fireplace, and artefacts of Dirk's travels prominently displayed on the mantelpiece.

It was late afternoon, and already growing dark when they arrived. They had made several stops along the way. Dirk had shown her his old home in Pacific Grove, the beach at Santa Cruz, and they had had a late leisurely lunch in Carmel.

While Dirk carried their bags up, Nicole went to the window to gaze at the sparkling lights of the city and the bridges. In just a few minutes she heard the door shut and sensed his presence in the room. He came up behind her and put his arms around her, bending his head down to lay his cheek against hers.

'Well, what do you think?'

'I love it,' she said.

She twisted her head around so that she could look up into his eyes, glistening brightly in the dim room. His hold on her tightened, and his lips began to play lightly, teasingly, with hers in nipping, grazing kisses, the tip of his tongue outlining the contours of her mouth.

'Lord, how I've ached for you this past week, Nicole,' he ground out. 'It's been torture to be so close to you and not be able to touch you like this.'

'I know,' she whispered.

As his hands began to move across the front of her sweater, just skimming her breasts, her blood grew heated and her heart started to pound. She drew in a sharp breath and closed her eyes, pressing herself back against his body, instantly aware as she did so that he was as aroused as she was.

'I love you, darling,' his breath came hotly in her ear. 'And I want you—now!'

His hand slipped underneath the thin sweater and travelled upwards over her bare midriff, her ribcage, to settle firmly at last on her breast. As he moulded her softness, the lacy bra slid sensuously over her skin, sending charges of electricity through her whole body. Then the kiss deepened, urgent now, demanding, penetrating.

When she couldn't endure another moment of the near-painful pleasure, she twisted around in his arms to face him. With his green eyes burning into hers, he slowly raised the sweater over her head, pulled it off and dropped it on a chair. As he fumbled with the front clasp of her bra, she could sense the explosive pent-up energy within him, barely held in check.

After drawing the wispy material over her shoulders to join the discarded sweater, he came back to cover her bare breasts with his hands, exploring every soft curve, his sensitive fingers moving in circles until they reached the taut, thrusting peaks.

'I'd forgotten how beautiful you are,' he said softly as his eyes drank in her nakedness. Then he smiled crookedly and took her in his arms. 'I'm afraid I only have one bedroom,' he murmured.

'What a shame,' Nicole replied dreamily.

'But it's a very big bed.'

She drew her head back and smiled up at him. 'Shall we try it, then, to see if I fit?'

Dirk bent down to swoop her up in his arms and carried her down a short hallway. With her arms twined around his neck, she laid her head on his shoulder, filled with delicious anticipation. In a moment, he nudged a door open with one foot, and she opened her eyes to a darkened bedroom, with only the street lights outside casting streaky shafts of light into the room for illumination.

Dirk set her carefully down on the bed and quickly stripped off his own clothing. She lay there gazing up at him, entranced at each new revelation of the strong, muscular body. When he had finished, he knelt down beside her and pulled off her trousers until she lay naked before him. He lifted his head and simply gazed down at her for several moments without touching her.

Then slowly, lingeringly, he began to stroke her, from her neck and shoulders down to her toes. As his mouth followed, she clutched at the dark head, holding it to her. The feel of his skin under her fingers, the taut muscles quivering under her touch, the clean, soapy scent of him, filled her with an aching desire, until finally, with a groan, he raised up and covered her body with his.

The week flew by. They took in all the sights of the fascinating city by the bay, strolled around the beautiful Japanese Tea Garden in Golden Gate Park, had dinner at Fishermen's Wharf, rode the cable cars and explored the arts and crafts shops at Sausalito, across the Golden Gate Bridge in Marin County.

Each day passed in a pleasant whirl of activity, each night in an exciting blur of passion, and as the week progressed Nicole had fallen more deeply in love with Dirk than ever. Every new thing she learned about him only convinced her that she wanted to spend the rest of her life with this man, no matter what.

Except for their more civilised surroundings, it was as though they were back in the cabin at Glacier Park again. They created a little world of their own, a world of companionship as well as love, where they soon discovered that they both harboured a secret, almost guilty passion for bluegrass music, old Hollywood musicals and seafood of every description.

Most important, however, was the way Nicole blossomed under Dirk's expert lovemaking, which was exquisitely tender one moment, almost out of control with desire the next. She gave herself to him completely during those hours of passion, trusting, vulnerable, secure in his love.

By the end of the week, her whole life in Beverly Hills began to seem like the dream, and Dirk's world the reality. The few times she thought about it, she still hoped he would take the job with her father's company, but it seemed less important to her each day, each hour, spent alone with him.

They still hadn't spoken of it. On Monday, they'd driven down the peninsula to Palo Alto for Dirk's meeting with his department head at Stanford, but all he said when it was over was that the terms of the spring teaching post had been spelled out, but that he still hadn't come to any definite decision.

Finally it was Saturday, the week almost over. Tomorrow Dirk would drive her home and they would make plans for the future. Although it was a foregone conclusion that it would be together, it was still up in the air just where that would be.

That morning at breakfast Dirk dropped his bombshell and announced that he had planned a small gathering in the apartment that night so that Nicole could meet some of his closest friends.

'Just five or six people,' he said.

They were sitting at the small table in his sunny kitchen having a last cup of coffee. Dirk had lit one of his rare cigarettes and was lounging contentedly back in his chair, his long legs apart. He wore only a worn, faded pair of blue jeans, leaving his chest and shoulders bare.

Nicole, still in her dressing-gown, stared at him, her cup halfway to her mouth. 'Oh, Dirk!' she said, dismayed. 'On our last night!'

'Don't worry, it'll be all right. Most of them have small children and will want to get home to them early.' He stubbed out his cigarette and leaned across the table to take her hand. He raised it and placed his lips on the palm. 'We have a whole lifetime ahead of us, darling,' he murmured. 'I want to show you off.'

She was so moved by this small gesture of affection, and so touched by his assumption that their future was definitely going to be together, that she would have agreed to anything. Besides, she had to admit she was curious to meet his friends.

'Well, all right,' she said. 'What should I wear?'

He threw back his head and laughed. 'Just like a woman!' he exclaimed. 'The right clothes will solve anything.' He gave her a fond look. 'It doesn't matter. It's a pretty eclectic bunch. You could show up in a gunny sack and outshine every other woman there. But, if you're really worried about it, I'd say keep it casual.'

*   *   *

That evening, while Dirk was in the kitchen setting out the food, Nicole went into his bedroom to get ready. As she sat on the bed surveying the clothes she had hung in his wardrobe, she had to wonder just what 'casual' meant in his circle. She'd brought her red velvet dress, just in case, but that seemed a little too formal.

Dirk himself had on a pair of dark trousers and a white dress shirt, unbuttoned at the neck, the sleeves rolled up, looking as elegant as he had in his dinner jacket. How casual was that? Finally she decided on a plain but beautifully cut off-white silk dress with a low square neckline and straight skirt. A pair of high-heeled sandals and her antique pearl earrings would give it a slightly more dressy touch.

When she was through dressing, she pinned her long dark hair up in a sleek chignon, applied a deft touch of make up and surveyed her reflection in the mirror with satisfaction. She could go anywhere, meet anyone the way she looked now.

She went into the kitchen, where Dirk was standing at the counter with his back to her, engrossed in tossing a salad. To her surprise she had learned during the past week that he was something of a gourmet cook, and the few meals he'd fixed for her were a far cry from the beans and bacon they'd had as a steady diet at the cabin.

'Anything I can do to help?' she asked.

'Nope. Everything's under control.' He turned around, smiling, but in the next instant the smile faded, and a frown slowly began to darken his features. 'Hell, Nicole,' he said, 'you've pinned your hair up again. I hope it isn't all gooey with that spray stuff.'

Stricken, she raised a hand to her head. 'Should I go change it?' she asked.

At that moment the doorbell rang. Wiping his hands on a towel, Dirk came to her side, put an arm around her and kissed her lightly on the nose.

'It's too late now. Don't worry about it. You look great.'

By the middle of the evening, it was perfectly clear to Nicole that the party was a total disaster. Her jaws ached from smiling and her throat was tight from forcing out the inane platitudes that were her only attempts at conversation.

It had all gone terribly wrong. To begin with, her clothes, her hair, everything about her was out of place. The minute the first guests arrived, the meaning of that last troubled look Dirk had given her became instantly clear.

Of the four other women present, three of them wives of Dirk's associates, the other his assistant at the university, only one of them even had on a skirt, and that looked as though it had been whipped up that afternoon out of an old ragged pair of blue jeans. The other three, including Janet Ainsley, Dirk's red-haired assistant, were dressed in worn denims and mannish shirts, and looked as though they were ready for a hike in the woods instead of a party.

Nicole stood stiffly by the fireplace in the living-room, sipping her wine, the artificial little smile still plastered on her face like a mask, and watching the others, who were all grouped in a tight little semicircle around Dirk. Although there were ten other

people present, counting Dirk, she had never felt
so alone.

They all hated her, that much was evident. With
her sleek hairstyle, her clever make-up, her simple
elegant dress, her pearls, she might have come from
Mars for all she had in common with the other
women. Not one of them had on even a trace of
lipstick, their hair looked as though they'd simply
washed it and combed it out, and they all had intense, intelligent expressions on their faces as they
discussed the latest discoveries in wildlife be-
haviour in highly technical terms.

To be fair, Dirk had made an effort to include
Nicole, even praising her for her adaptation to the
primitive conditions at the cabin, but each story he
told—or worse, insisted she tell herself—only made
her sound more clumsy, more inept, more cloddish.
They'd all had a good laugh at the bear episode,
the meals she'd ruined, the way she'd shrunk Dirk's
shirts.

As she watched the close-knit little group, hot
tears of self-pity smarted behind her eyes, particularly at the sight of Janet Ainsley, who was sitting
on the couch so close to Dirk that she'd be in his
lap in another moment. In spite of the fact that the
redhead made not the slightest concession to
grooming or fashion, she was a very attractive
woman, even beautiful, with that flaming mane of
auburn hair, wide china-blue eyes and slim, ath-
letic figure.

She could also talk to him knowledgeably about
his work, and that was the part that really hurt. At
the moment she had her startling blue eyes fixed
adoringly on Dirk, as he and one of the other men

carried on a heated discussion, bandying Latin nomenclature about, so that Nicole couldn't even guess the subject.

She knew that if she didn't do something quickly she'd burst into tears in front of the whole company and really disgrace herself. She turned around to stare down into the low flickering fire and drained her glass of wine. Maybe she should plead a headache. Or faint. Or get drunk! Anything to get out of that room, away from these people.

Then she heard a woman's voice at her side. 'I'm afraid all this must be very boring for you, Nicole.'

Hastily Nicole trotted out her fake smile and turned to see Rhoda Lambert, the wife of one of Dirk's teaching associates. She was fortyish, with short dark hair streaked with grey, and the expression on her face was warm, friendly, and tinged with pity.

Nicole gave a brittle laugh. 'Well, I'll have to admit I don't really understand what they're talking about.'

'I know. I was the same way when Jack and I were first married. Scientists can be very selfish and inconsiderate when it comes to their work. It's really all they live for, and when they get together the rest of the world simply ceases to exist.'

'I'm beginning to find that out. Doesn't it bother you?'

'Oh, I'm used to it by now,' Rhoda replied with a wry twist to her mouth.

'How long have you been married?' asked Nicole.

'It'll be fifteen years in May.'

'Do you have children?'

'Yes, we have two. A boy twelve and a girl ten.'

'And does your husband go off on these long field trips too?'

'He used to, but he gave it up a few years ago. Nowadays he teaches full time.'

Nicole laughed. 'You mean you finally convinced him to give it up?'

Rhoda shook her head. 'No, it wasn't that. Actually, he got tired of it himself. When he turned forty he just decided he'd had enough of field research, that it was time to let the younger men take over, men like Dirk.'

'I'm sure that was a great relief. It must have been hard for you, trying to make a home, raising small children, with your husband gone so much.'

'Oh, we always went with him,' said Rhoda. 'It was a marvellous education for the children. Me too, as a matter of fact. It can be done,' she added softly. 'You proved that for yourself when you were snowbound up there in Montana and couldn't get out. You survived, and it sounds as though you learned a lot from the experience.'

Rhoda's sympathy and encouragement gave a real lift to Nicole's flagging spirits. In just a few years Dirk would be forty. Maybe he'd be ready to give it up then too, and she could convince her father to renew his offer of a job. It was a cheering thought.

The group had broken up now. While Dirk went into the kitchen for a fresh bottle of wine, Janet Ainsley got up from the couch and came over to the two women by the fireplace.

'Well, Nicole,' she said, 'what do you think of our little group? I hope you don't find us too boring. Or,' she added with a meaningful glance that swept Nicole up and down, 'too primitive.'

'Not at all,' Nicole replied pleasantly. 'Whatever is important to Dirk is important to me too.'

Janet turned to the older woman. 'How have you been, Rhoda?' she asked.

'Great. And you?'

'Oh, working hard,' the redhead said with a mock sigh. 'I was hoping Dirk would be here for the spring semester to help supervise getting his data organised, but it looks as though I'll be on my own when I get back from my vacation.' She turned to Nicole. 'He never did finish his work at Glacier, you know.'

Nicole bridled at the accusing tone. Janet made it sound as though it was all *her* fault. 'Well, it was his choice, after all,' she said sweetly.

Janet returned an equally saccharine smile. 'Yes, but isn't it great that he's decided to go back to the park next month to finish up after all?'

Nicole's whole body stiffened against the shockwaves that threatened to engulf her. Her head started to spin crazily, the pit of her stomach felt as though it had just fallen out, and it took every ounce of will-power she possessed to control the violent tremor that rocked through her.

Dimly, as though from a great distance, she heard the two women discussing Dirk's plans, plans he had obviously made without consulting her. He hadn't even had the decency to inform her of his decision before broadcasting it to the world.

He'd *promised* her! Her fingernails dug into the palms of her hands as she clenched them into fists to stop the uncontrollable tremor. She'd trusted him, and he'd broken his word to her.

Just then Dirk came back from the kitchen carrying the fresh bottle of wine. After setting it down on the coffee-table, he wandered over to the three women and put an arm around Nicole's rigid shoulders.

'How's it going?' he asked, hugging her to him. 'Is Rhoda filling you in on all the tribulations of life with a mad scientist?'

Nicole was torn between screaming at him, or bursting into tears and rushing from the room. Or, better yet, turning on him and cracking her hand across his fatuous, grinning face.

As it turned out, she didn't have to decide, since Rhoda, as though sensing trouble, rushed in to break the tense silence.

'Dirk, Janet mentioned that you'll be going back to Glacier next month. When are you leaving?'

It was, of course, the worst possible subject to mention, but there was no way Rhoda could have known that. Nicole felt Dirk's hand tighten on her shoulder, his body grow stiff at her side. No one said a word.

Then, as if on cue, the telephone rang.

'Excuse me,' murmured Dirk with patent relief, and went into the hall to answer it.

When he came back, a few minutes later, Janet Ainsley was waiting for him at the door, and the two of them spent the next half-hour deep in what appeared to be a very serious conversation. By then it was too late to confront him, and all Nicole could do was bide her time until the others left.

The rest of the evening passed in a blur. She was still seething inwardly, and the wine she consumed steadily, one glass after another, was the only thing that kept her from attacking Dirk right then and there and creating a scene in front of the whole group.

He seemed perfectly at ease, just as though nothing had happened, laughing and joking with his friends, trying to draw Nicole into the conversation. Even he, however, thick-headed and insensitive as he was, knew something was up, and kept darting her worried little glances.

Finally the hideous evening came to an end. When the last guest had been ushered out, the last goodbye echoing down the hall, Dirk closed the door and turned to her. But, before he could get a word out, she marched up to him and thrust her face up close to his.

'You bastard!' she ground out. 'You absolute swine!'

'Now, just hold on a minute, Nicole,' he said. 'I can explain everything.'

She gave him a withering look. 'Oh, please, do,' she drawled sarcastically. 'I'm really dying to hear just why you decided to tell that—that *redhead* you were going back to Montana before you felt it necessary to confide your plans to *me*!' He opened his mouth, but she cut him short, fuelled by her anger. 'I suppose she's going with you. Maybe you plan to have a pleasant little interlude with her the way you did with me. Or perhaps it's already been going on for some time.'

He grabbed her by the shoulders, his fingers digging into her flesh. 'Stop it, Nicole!' he barked.

'Just stop it right now! You don't know what you're saying.'

'Oh?' she said with a lift of one eyebrow. 'Was she lying, then? She's obviously in love with you. Maybe she made it all up.' She folded her arms across her chest and glared at him. 'I just want to know one thing, Dirk. Did you or did you not tell Janet Ainsley that you were going back to Glacier?'

He dropped his hands from her shoulders in a gesture of defeat. 'All right, I admit I was wrong to say anything to Janet. However——'

'You were wrong even to make the decision without consulting me!' Nicole broke in angrily. 'Dirk, you promised! You said we'd talk it over. You knew how much it meant to me.'

'But I hadn't really made a definite decision.'

'Then why did you tell Janet?'

'I told Janet I *might* go. She's leaving on her vacation early tomorrow morning, and there were some things she had to know about the project in *case* I decided to go to Montana before she got back.'

'I see,' Nicole said stiffly. 'Then you're saying that you haven't definitely made up your mind yet.'

'Well, as a matter of fact, I have,' he said defensively. 'I'd planned to discuss it with you as soon as the others left.'

'What's to discuss?' she cried dramatically. 'If you've made up your mind already, it sounds to me as though it's a little late for any discussion.' She eyed him accusingly. 'You never once seriously considered my father's offer, did you?'

Dirk frowned and stared down at the floor for several long moments. His silence was all the answer

Nicole needed. She was so angry, felt so betrayed, that she couldn't stand to be in the same room with him another second. With a little cry, she turned on her heel and marched purposefully away from him.

In the bedroom, she yanked her suitcase out of the wardrobe and slammed it down on the bed. She was already throwing her clothes and personal belongings into it when Dirk appeared in the doorway. He stood there glumly, his hands in his trouser pockets, leaning against the wall, watching her for a few minutes without speaking.

Then he shoved himself away from the wall and came over to stand by the side of the bed. He grabbed her by the arm and forced her around to face him.

'What are you doing?' he demanded in a low voice.

'What does it look like I'm doing? I'm packing my bag. Then I'm going to call a cab to take me to the airport. Then I'm going to sit there until I can get a flight home.'

'Don't you think you're being a little unreasonable? I'm going to drive you home tomorrow, remember? I thought that would give us time to talk, to make some plans.'

Nicole glared up at him. 'What plans? *Your* plans, isn't that what you mean?' She twisted her arm out of his grasp and resumed her packing, tossing her things inside the bag helter-skelter. 'What I don't understand,' she muttered, 'is why you didn't tell me days ago that you weren't going to take that job with my father. It would have saved us both a lot of trouble.'

'The reason I didn't tell you was that I hadn't really decided. You'd asked me to think it over, and that's what I was doing. Nicole, I'd be a fish out of water in your father's company. I don't belong in the corporate world. I'd be miserable, and I certainly wouldn't be any good at it.'

'Well, you could have given it a try!' she cried, turning to face him again. 'And, talking about fish out of water, how do you think I felt tonight, with your friends all sitting around giving me those *looks*! Passing judgement on me, as though I were some kind of intruder.'

'How hard did you try to fit in?' he countered angrily. 'They're good people, and they wanted to like you. You wouldn't even give them a chance.'

'Why should I? They had their minds all made up the minute they set eyes on me, before I even opened my mouth. Especially that redhead. She hated me on sight. Just give me one good reason why I should have gone out of my way for them.'

'For the same reason I put on that damned dinner-jacket and went to *your* friends' party, that's why!' Dirk rejoined hotly. He gave an exasperated sigh. 'Lord, Nicole, you're the limit! You're acting like the same spoilt brat I picked up out of the snow.'

She slammed her suitcase shut viciously. 'Thank you,' she said. 'Then you'll be glad to be rid of me. Maybe you should have left me there in the first place.'

She heard his sharp intake of breath, then there was dead silence in the room while she struggled with the snaps of her overstuffed bag.

'All right, Nicole,' he said at last in a resigned tone of voice. 'If you want to leave, that's your decision. I love you, and I want to marry you. But I can't fit myself into your world. I'd only be half a man if I sold myself to your father and his cronies. What's more, I'm not so sure you're really happy in it yourself. What earthly good is it to you? You were a different person in the midst of all that phoney glitter. You spend your days in idleness, half bored out of your mind in meaningless activity.'

Nicole turned to him. 'And what am I supposed to do in your world?' she challenged. 'Sit at home knitting while you roam around the world looking for bears?'

'No, of course not!' he said. 'I'd want you to come with me, to share it with me.'

'And what about a home? A family?'

'Other people do it. Rhoda has managed quite well all these years. So have a lot of other wives. You coped with it yourself, and it was the best thing that ever happened to you.'

'If you don't mind, I think I know what's best for me. *You* certainly don't want to hear any advice about what I think is best for you, so let me be the judge of that.'

He stared down at her, his face pinched and white. 'If that's the kind of life you want,' he ground out, 'maybe you should marry this Victor character your father is so in love with.'

Nicole lifted her chin. 'Well, maybe I will!'

He gave her a pleading look and raised a hand towards her. 'Nicole,' he said softly, 'I'll say it one more time. I love you. I want to marry you. Doesn't that mean anything to you?'

At his obviously heartfelt words, her anger began to drain away, only to be replaced with a sense of dull hopelessness. 'It used to mean everything to me,' she replied in a strained voice. 'But I can't marry a man who makes the most crucial decision of his life without even taking the trouble to consult me.'

She lifted up her bag and set it on the floor. In another minute she'd start to cry, and she couldn't bear the thought of doing that. Biting her lip so hard that she drew blood, just to hold back the tears, she turned from him and went over to the wardrobe to get her coat.

Dirk didn't say another word, but even before she had slipped the coat off its hanger she heard his footsteps moving away from her out of the room, down the hall, then the front door as it slammed behind him.

It was then that she collapsed on the bed and let the tears fall freely.

CHAPTER NINE

NICOLE sat in the bay window of her bedroom staring out at the driving rain pouring out of a leaden sky. It was the first of March, over a month since her flight from San Francisco, away from Dirk, from what she had hoped was to be her happiness.

Since she'd been back she hadn't heard one word from him, or even about him. She still shuddered when she recalled that taxi ride from his apartment, the long wait for a flight to Los Angeles, and then the dismal plane trip in the middle of the night.

When she had finally arrived home, physically and emotionally exhausted, her father had just come down for breakfast. He took one look at her dishevelled figure, opened his mouth to quiz her, then snapped it shut.

'I'm home, Father,' she'd said wearily. 'For good.'

He'd only nodded, and since then the subject had never even been discussed between them.

The telephone rang shrilly, breaking into her glum reverie. Nicole jumped up, ran over to the bedside table and snatched it up. It could be him. She didn't know for sure he'd gone back to the cabin.

'Hello,' she said eagerly.

'Hi,' came Margot's voice.

'Oh, hello, Margot.' Nicole sank down on the side of the bed. 'What's up?'

'I thought you might like to have lunch at the club with me today. My treat. There's going to be a fashion show, all the latest from New York and Paris.'

'I don't know, Margot. It's such a rotten day, I don't feel much like going out.'

'Now you listen to me, Nicole West,' her friend said sternly. 'It's time you began to face a few facts and started living again. Ever since you broke off your engagement to Dirk Morgan——'

'It wasn't a real engagement,' Nicole broke in. 'And besides, I don't want to talk about it.'

'Well, you'd darned well *better* talk about it!' Margot exploded. 'If not to me, to someone. How long do you think you can go on like this, hiding yourself away in your room, not going out, not seeing anyone? You're headed for trouble, Nicole, if you don't snap out of it soon.'

Nicole bridled, all ready to warn Margot to back off, to leave her alone, but before she could get the first word out a nagging little voice deep inside her told her that her friend was right. She couldn't go on like this. She wasn't eating properly, just picking at food that had no taste. She slept badly, and spent her days wandering aimlessly around the big house all by herself.

'All right, Margot,' she said with a sigh. 'You've made your point. I'll go to lunch with you today.'

'Such enthusiasm overwhelms me!' drawled Margot. 'How about one o'clock at the Palm Court?'

The fashionable dining-room at the tennis club was still crowded, but Margot had made a reservation ahead, and they were seated right away. The fashion show was still in progress, and as Nicole pushed lobster salad around her plate with her fork, she tried to work up some degree of interest in the models who paraded around the tables in one exclusive creation after another.

Margot had tried valiantly to make small talk for the first half-hour, but even she gave up when all the response she got was monosyllables and false smiles. Finally, over coffee, she set her spoon down in her saucer with such a loud clang that Nicole gazed over at her in alarm.

'Now you listen to me,' said Margot, leaning across the table and fixing Nicole with a grim look. 'I've just about had it with you. Are you going to tell me what happened and get it off your chest once and for all, or am I going to have to beat it out of you?'

Nicole had to smile at the truly determined expression on her friend's face. 'Would you do that, Margot?' she asked.

'If you recall, I was always bigger and stronger than you when we were in school. I did it then, and I can do it now,' Margot added with a grin. Then she sobered. 'Have you heard from him?'

Nicole shook her head. 'No, and I don't expect to.'

'Is it really over for good?'

'Afraid so.'

'Well, you know the saying, "Men have died from time to time and worms have eaten them, but not for love."'

Nicole gave her a wry smile. 'Do you believe that?'

Margot shrugged. 'I don't know. I've been in love so many times I've lost count, and I'm still here. There's another saying I like much better. "Off with the old love and on with the new." I think it's time you found out there were other men in the world. That's the best medicine for a broken heart.'

But before Nicole could answer a shadow fell across their table, and she looked up to see Victor Channing standing there. She hadn't seen him or heard from him since the party at the Campbells', and she was surprised to see him now.

'Hello, Victor,' she said coolly. 'What in the world are you doing here at a fashion show?'

'I was having lunch in the bar when I happened to see you and Margot sitting in here. May I join you?'

Margot jumped hurriedly to her feet, dropping her napkin in the process. 'Sure, Victor,' she said. 'I was just going to the powder-room. Be right back, Nicole.'

With that she was gone. Victor sat down at the empty chair between them, raised a hand, and a waiter came rushing over. While Victor ordered a cup of coffee, Nicole leaned back in her chair with a sigh of resignation. She was stuck with him now, and wondered if Margot had set her up.

'How have you been, Nicole?' he asked, when the steaming cup of coffee was set before him. 'I haven't seen you for ages.'

'No,' she replied, idly toying with her spoon. 'I've been sticking pretty close to home.'

'You haven't been ill, have you? You look a little pale.'

She shook her head. 'No, I'm fine.'

They sat in silence for a while, drinking their coffee, and watching the parade of models. Finally he set his cup down and gave her a direct look.

'There's a new production of *Aida* at the opera house on Saturday night,' he said slowly. 'Would you care to go with me?'

'Victor,' she said with a slight frown, 'there really isn't any point in——'

He held up a hand to stop her. 'No strings,' he said hastily. 'We're old friends, Nicole. I enjoy your company, and we both like opera. That's all.'

Nicole debated inwardly. Although she'd never been in love with Victor, and had strenuously resisted marrying him, now that the pressure from her father was off she had to admit there really wasn't anything wrong with him. He was a decent person, and he was right. They were old friends. They came from the same world, knew the same people, enjoyed the same things.

'All right,' she said at last. 'So long as you understand how I feel about——' She broke off with a shrug. 'You know.'

'I do. And I respect your feelings.' He drained his coffee and rose to his feet. 'Until Saturday, then. I'll pick you up around seven o'clock.'

To Nicole's surprise, the evening out with Victor passed quite pleasantly. Although she wasn't as ardent a fan of the opera as he was, it gave her spirits a definite lift just to get dressed up and pay attention to her appearance once again. In the long weeks since she had left Dirk in San Francisco, she'd let herself slip into disgraceful grooming habits.

When she had told her father she was going to the opera with Victor on Saturday, he'd restrained himself admirably and merely nodded. But she could tell he was both surprised and pleased at this sudden unexpected turn of events by the small smile of satisfaction he couldn't quite hide.

True to his word, throughout the whole evening, Victor had behaved towards her exactly as he'd promised. He'd said 'No strings,' and he'd meant it. He treated her with elaborate courtesy, kept his distance from her, and in fact hardly touched her except to help her on and off with her coat.

Once Nicole was reassured that he didn't mean to press her romantically, she found she could relax around him more, even enjoy his company. At this low point in her life, anything familiar was very comforting.

Somehow, after that first Saturday night at the opera, they fell into the habit of going everywhere together. In less than a week, hostesses even began asking them to parties as a couple. So long as they could remain on strictly friendly terms, this didn't bother Nicole. In fact, she even came to depend upon it.

But most of all there was the enormous advantage of having less time to think. She deliberately filled every minute of each day with shopping, luncheons, teas, bridge games, hairdresser's appointments, just as Victor filled her nights with dances, concerts and formal dinners.

She even started sleeping better, falling into bed exhausted each night from the constant round of social events. There was almost a frantic quality to the way she threw herself into this whirl of activity, as though if she stopped running, stopped to catch her breath, something dreadful would happen to her.

She still hadn't heard anything from Dirk, or even anything about him, nor did she expect to, and she congratulated herself that she was over him at last.

Then suddenly, after about three weeks of this, Victor called her early one evening just as she was getting dressed to go out to a dinner party with him.

'I'm sorry, Nicole,' he said, 'I won't be able to make it for our dinner date. An emergency has come up in our Houston office, and I've got to leave tonight.'

Nicole felt a sinking feeling in the pit of her stomach. 'How long will you be gone?' she asked.

'Only a few days. I'll call you as soon as I get back.'

After she had hung up, she stood by the side of the bed in her bra and lacy black half-slip, fighting off the waves of panic that threatened. She started pacing the room, padding barefoot from one end to the other, wringing her hands, hugging her bare arms, resisting the tears of weakness welling up behind her eyes.

After a while she sank down slowly on the bed and sat there, rigid, staring into space. 'What's wrong with me?' she whispered aloud.

Surely her reaction was totally out of proportion to the provocation? Why should it make this much difference to her that Victor would be gone for a few days? Was she falling in love with him? She shook her head vigorously. She had come to depend on him, even to enjoy his company, but the mere idea of anything more was totally repellent to her.

She lay back on the pillows and closed her eyes, trying to force herself to relax. Immediately a picture of Dirk rose up in her mind, followed by a veritable panorama of remembered aspects of the man. Dirk at the cabin, bearded and dressed in his heavy outdoor clothes chopping wood. Dirk patiently teaching her how to light the gas stove. Dirk seated at his desk poring over his maps and charts. Dirk in his formal evening wear at the Campbells' party.

Most poignant of all was the memory of his face looming over hers during their lovemaking, the light of desire gleaming in the speckled green eyes. And last, his tight-lipped face as she had hurled accusations at him that last night at his apartment.

Groaning aloud, she twisted her body around to bury her face in the pillows, as the dam finally burst and the great sobs were wrenched out of her. It was Dirk's face, the fresh clean scent of his skin and hair, the feel of his arms around her, his hungry mouth on hers, that she had been fighting off all these weeks in her manic attempts to fill every minute of her life.

After she'd cried herself out, she raised up on one elbow and looked dazedly around the room. It had grown dark outside, and the lamppost out in the garden shed gloomy shadows into every corner.

Nicole reached out and switched on the bedside lamp, then scrambled off the bed and went into the bathroom. After splashing cold water on her face, she began slowly and methodically to repair her make-up. She'd just have to go to the party without Victor.

* * *

He came back to town, as promised, two days later, and called her immediately.

'If you're not busy tonight, would you have dinner with me?'

Nicole was very glad to hear from him. Although she had kept busy during the time he was gone, it wasn't the same thing attending social functions unescorted.

'Yes,' she said, 'I'd like that. I've been invited to a dinner party at the Campbells', but I'm sure it would be all right with them if I brought you along.'

There was a short silence at the other end of the line. Then he said, 'Would you mind very much if we just went alone to the club? I'm pretty knocked out, and don't feel like too much company.'

'No, of course not,' she replied.

Victor was strangely silent all during dinner, hardly even making his usual polite efforts at conversation. Although he did look tired, Nicole had the feeling there was more to it than that. In fact, the minute he had suggested dinner alone, her defences were on the alert.

When they had finished dinner and had been served their coffee, he sat staring down into his cup, stirring his spoon around and around in it. Finally he raised his head.

'Nicole, I want to tell you how much I've enjoyed being with you these past several weeks.'

'I've enjoyed it too, Victor,' she said brightly. Somehow she knew what was coming, but there was no way she could stop it.

'And,' he went on, 'I've honoured our original agreement that there were to be no strings.' He shrugged diffidently. 'No romantic involvement.'

'Yes, you have, and I've really appreciated it,' she said with feeling.

'Well, I'm going to break that agreement now.'

'Victor——' she said in a warning tone.

He held up a hand. 'It's got to be said, Nicole. You can't have it all your way. I've played your game. You owe it to me to at least hear me out.'

She slumped back in her chair with a sigh. He was right, of course. 'All right,' she said.

'As you've no doubt guessed by now, I still want to marry you,' he announced without preamble. 'And, before you say anything, I feel it's only fair to tell you that, at this point, it's either that or nothing.'

'I see,' she replied slowly. 'You mean that if I don't agree to marry you we won't see each other any more.'

He nodded. 'It has to be that way, Nicole. Don't you see that?'

'Yes,' she agreed reluctantly. 'Yes, I guess I do.'

'Well?'

Nicole bit her lip as she pondered the alternatives. One thing seemed clear: she couldn't marry Victor. The very idea was distasteful to her. She simply didn't love him. She never would, not the way she'd loved Dirk.

She looked at him. He was no Adonis, but, on the other hand neither was he repulsive. His sandy hair was thinning and he was starting to put on weight, but most women would jump at the chance to marry him. He was rich, cultivated, intelligent, courteous, and they had so much in common.

He was watching her carefully, sipping his coffee, waiting for her answer.

'Will you give me a little time to think it over?' she asked at last.

'How long?' was the prompt response.

'A week.'

'All right—one week.' He pushed his chair back. 'Shall we go now? I'd like to turn in early tonight.'

When Nicole got home, at a far earlier hour than usual, on her way to her room she noticed that the light was on in her father's study. On an impulse, she rapped lightly on the door.

'Come in,' came his voice.

She opened the door and stepped inside. He was sitting in his favourite leather easy chair reading, and he looked up in some surprise when he saw her standing there.

'What brings you home so early?' he asked.

'Oh, Victor was tired from his trip to Houston. We had dinner at the club, then decided to make an early night of it.'

He waited, still watching her. She went over to his desk and, as she started to spin the large globe slowly around, she could feel his eyes on her. Finally she turned around to face him, leaning her hips back against the desk.

'He asked me to marry him again tonight,' she announced.

Her father raised an eyebrow and carefully set his book face down on the table beside his chair. 'Surely that doesn't come as any surprise to you?'

Nicole shrugged. 'I was hoping we could go on as we have, just being friends.'

He gave a low chuckle. 'Still thinking you can have it all your way, aren't you, Nicole?'

She stared at him. 'What's that supposed to mean?'

'Come and sit down,' he said, pointing to the chair next to his. When she was seated beside him, he leaned towards her, his face grave. 'What did you tell him?'

'I asked him to give me some time.'

'Do you love him?'

Nicole goggled at the unexpected question. To her knowledge, her father had never thought twice about her feelings, or was even aware she had any. Appearances were all that ever mattered to him.

'No,' she said, 'of course not. I never have.'

'It would make a good marriage. There are many different kinds of love, you know. A marriage based on common interests and background can be very successful, sometimes even more so than one based on passion.'

She gave him a sharp look. 'Is that the kind of marriage you and Mother had?'

A sad, far-away look clouded his features, and he shook his head slowly. 'No, it wasn't. I loved your mother, and she loved me.' He laughed. 'Hard to believe, I know, but for the short time we had together we were very happy.'

'Then why are you advising me to marry without love?'

He raised his eyebrows. 'Did I do that? Think about it, Nicole. I only said such a marriage *could* work. I wasn't necessarily recommending it.'

'I thought you were so mad to have me marry Victor. In fact, we had quite a heated discussion about that very subject when we went to Glacier last fall.' She laughed wryly. 'In fact, it's how I got lost in that snowstorm in the first place.'

'True,' he replied musingly. 'But things have changed since then.'

'What things?' she asked sharply.

He shrugged. 'Well, one reason I was pushing your marriage to Victor was that I'd come to the conclusion that you were incapable of falling in love. I blamed myself. I'd spoilt you, given you every material thing you'd ever wanted, but had never really taken the trouble to make you face some of the harder facts of life. I just assumed a marriage of convenience was the best you could expect.' He gave her a direct, penetrating look. 'Then Dirk Morgan came along.'

Nicole looked hurriedly away. 'That's all over,' she muttered. 'There's no point even discussing it.'

'Are you so sure?' her father asked mildly.

She turned to face him. 'What are you saying? Don't you realise what happened? Surely you're aware that he turned down that job with you?'

'I know. He wrote me a very courteous note telling me that, and spelling out his reasons. Which, by the way, I respect. That young man knows what he wants, and nothing's going to stop him. It's a quality I've always admired.'

'Father!' she cried, aghast. 'I thought you'd be furious with him! I know I was.'

'Why?' he enquired pleasantly. 'Was it because he disappointed me, or because he didn't prostrate himself at your feet to do your bidding?'

'Well, no,' she spluttered, 'of course not! The reason I was so upset was that he made the decision without consulting me. Not only that, but he told that redheaded assistant of his first.'

Her father nodded owlishly. 'Ah, I see—the green-eyed monster rears its ugly head!'

'Are you implying I was jealous?'

'Well? Weren't you?' He reached over to take her hand in his. 'Nicole, you're a lovely girl, beautiful, intelligent, a *nice* girl, in every possible way, except one.' He smiled. 'You can't stand to be crossed in any way.'

'But he *promised* we'd talk it over before he made up his mind!' she cried. 'And he broke that promise.'

'Well, all right, maybe he made a mistake, even an important one. Does that mean he quit loving you?'

'I can't believe this,' she said, shaking her head in bewilderment. 'The last thing I ever expected from you was a defence of Dirk Morgan. I thought you'd be out of your mind with joy at the mere fact that I was even *considering* marrying Victor.'

'What I want,' he said in measured tones, 'is for you to be happy, to fulfil the best that's in you. Marriage to Victor would be no different from what you have right now. It was Dirk Morgan who brought out your best, who forced you to assume the responsibilities and obligations of a grown woman.'

Still stunned by this unexpected turn of events, Nicole could only stare down at the floor. Her father was actually saying the same thing Dirk had. She *was* a spoilt brat! She didn't really care whether he took the job with her father or not. She'd been far happier in that rough mountain cabin, opening cans and doing the housework, than she'd ever been living in the lap of luxury.

What she hadn't been able to tolerate was the fact that Dirk had made a decision without consulting her. He'd tried to explain to her that he'd felt obligated to at least let Janet Ainsley know there was a possibility he'd be going back to Glacier, but she had refused to listen. Not only had her precious pride been wounded, but her father was right again: she had been jealous.

Finally she looked at her father again. 'It doesn't matter anyway,' she said glumly. 'It's too late.'

'Are you sure?'

'Yes, I'm sure. When I left Dirk in San Francisco, I knew I was burning every bridge. I don't even know where he is.'

'He's at the cabin in Glacier Park,' he said smugly.

Her eyes flew open. 'How on earth do you know that?'

'I have my resources. I just thought it might be wise to keep track of him. I wasn't nearly as convinced as you were that it was really over between you. Ever since you came back, you've either been moping around the house or running around like a maniac just to fill up time.'

Nicole shook her head, lost in admiration. Still, it was too late. Surely Dirk had forgotten her by now?

'I don't think he wants me,' she said sadly.

'How do you know until you try?' Her father leaned towards her and fixed her with a stern look.

'Don't let your pride get in your way this time, Nicole. There's too much at stake.'

Three days later, Nicole stepped up into the helicopter at the tiny heliport in Cutbank, Montana, on the eastern edge of Glacier Park. Although it was still freezing cold, a bright sun glistened on the steep snow-covered Rocky Mountains, which loomed up majestically over the shabby little town.

Soon after they lifted off, the gabled roof of Many Glacier Hotel appeared up ahead, closed now until the first of May, and, behind it, the long icy blue finger of Swiftcurrent Lake. As she gazed down at the beautiful sight, all the glitter and glamour of the world she was leaving—her father's house, Beverly Hills society—began to fade from her mind.

She was nervous about the coming confrontation with Dirk, but filled also with a wild elation, a sense of adventure, of an irrevocable move from a life of illusion and appearances to one of solid reality.

She had purposely not radioed ahead to let him know she was coming. Gambling everything on this one throw of the dice, she had also instructed the helicopter pilot to take off again as soon as he set her down. Unless Dirk decided to turn her out in the snow, he'd have to take her in and listen to her.

It was late afternoon, the sun already starting to dip low towards the western peaks of the mountains. Nicole had flown into Helena, Montana, the night before, and early that morning hired a car and driver to take her to Cutbank, deliberately gauging her timing so that Dirk would be sure to have come back from the field.

The cabin was to the north and west of the hotel, quite some distance, and when she spotted the clearing, the small cabin itself, smoke rising up from it in the still air in greyish fluffy puffs, her heart suddenly missed a beat. What kind of reception she would get she hadn't the faintest idea.

As the helicopter descended towards the clearing, Nicole gathered up her things. Travelling light, she had only brought along necessary toilet articles and a few changes of simple clothing. That morning she'd washed her dark hair and combed it out loosely, letting it fall naturally to her shoulders, the way Dirk liked it. She had on his red shirt.

When they landed, the pilot didn't even shut off his engine. The minute he set down, Nicole shouted her thanks over the roar of the motor, then jumped out on to the crusty snow, ducking under the whirling rotors against the downdraught.

As soon as she was clear he took off again, and Nicole watched as he faded away into a mere black dot in the blue sky, the sound of the engine only a faint echo. She took a deep breath and turned towards the cabin, some fifty feet away.

Her heart gave one great lurch, then simply stopped beating when she saw Dirk standing in the doorway, obviously alerted by the sound of the helicopter. He didn't move, not one step towards her, not even a wave or a salute of greeting. He only stood there, tall and straight, his arms hanging loosely at his sides, his long legs slightly apart.

It was the longest fifty yards she had ever had to walk in her life. She had worn boots, but kept breaking through the thin crust of ice to the softer snow beneath it, and even though she picked her way carefully and kept her eyes fastened on her feet she stumbled several times over the difficult terrain.

Finally she came to a halt not three feet from him. He still hadn't moved a muscle, and when she looked up at him his face was drawn, the green eyes dull and hard. Now that she was actually here, she hadn't any idea what to say to him. She'd rehearsed several speeches since making the decision to come, but in the sheer impact of his actual physical presence they had all fled from her mind.

As she stared wordlessly up at him, his mouth twisted into a sardonic mocking smile and his eyes narrowed. 'What kind of game are you playing now, Nicole?' he asked in a low, toneless voice.

She lifted her chin and put on her brightest smile. 'I thought you might be looking for an assistant, and came to apply for the job.'

Dirk gazed into the distance over her head, frowning heavily, as though deep in thought. When he turned back to her, his expression seemed softer, slightly less forbidding.

'What can you do?' he asked.

'I can cook and clean. I can make log entries. I even know how to launder woollen shirts.'

Finally, unable to bear the tension a moment longer, she called his name and flung herself towards him. But before she could reach him he had gripped her hard by the arms, holding her at a distance from him.

'Damn you, Nicole,' he growled. 'Why did you come here?'

'I came to apologise, to explain, to... Oh, I don't know!' She gave him a stricken look. 'I came because I can't live without you.' She drew in a deep choking sob.

'Come on,' he said gruffly, pushing the door open. 'Let's go in. We'd better have a talk.'

Inside the cabin it was warm, a fire blazing on the stone hearth. Nicole took off her hat and gloves and jacket and looked around the familiar room. Nothing had changed. There was Dirk's desk, still littered with his notebooks, charts and maps. The same musty Indian blanket covered his bed. The same shabby couch sat in front of the fire.

Dirk was at the counter, his back to her, pouring brandy out into tin cups from the bottle he kept on the shelf. As she watched him, Nicole fought down the impulse to run over to him and throw her arms around him. He was right: they had to talk.

When he turned around, one hand outstretched with her drink, his gaze fell on the red shirt. His eyes widened, and for the first time he gave her a real smile. Suddenly she knew it would be all right. She had some fast talking to do, but that one smile was all it took to reassure her that she had done the right thing.

'Let's sit down,' he said.

She took her drink from him, and they settled themselves on the lumpy couch, he at one end, she at the other. They both took healthy swallows of the brandy before saying another word.

'Now,' said Dirk, setting his cup down on the floor, 'what's this all about?'

Nicole stared down at her hands, twisting them nervously in her lap, searching for a way to begin. 'Well, I had a talk with my father a few nights ago.'

He gave a short bark of a laugh. 'That must have been interesting, but I can't imagine how anything he had to say would bring you here.

She turned to face him. 'He pointed out a few unpleasant truths about his only child that made me not like her very much.'

He raised an eyebrow. 'Such as?'

'Oh, such as the fact that he'd spoilt me rotten, that I'd let my pride stop me from going after the one thing I really wanted.' Her voice broke. 'And that in his opinion you were the best thing that ever happened to me.' She gave him a tentative smile. 'Little things like that.'

Dirk put his elbows on his knees, cupping his face in his hands, and gazed into the fire. As Nicole watched the way the flickering flames played over his face, she felt a great surge of love for him. He was so *real*! Every feature, every lock of dark hair, every breath he took, was so dear to her that it almost choked her.

Finally he turned to look at her, grim-faced. 'It wasn't all your fault,' he said in a low voice. 'I did promise you not to make a decision about that blasted job without talking it over with you. To say the least, it was thoughtless of me to let even a hint of it slip to Janet first.' He heaved a deep sigh. 'Only I've been on my own for so long, and have never had anyone else to consider, that I just didn't think.'

'But if that's true, if you felt that way even after I left, why didn't you tell me? Why didn't you call, or write?'

'Because I'd already come to the unhappy conclusion even before that night that we could never make it work. Your reaction to what happened with Janet only confirmed it. You were happy in your world, and I was committed to mine. Neither of us could give in.'

'But I wasn't happy in my world!' she cried. 'After being with you, seeing what it meant to have a real purpose in life besides having fun or making money, I could never be satisfied with that empty existence again.'

'That's not true,' he said insistently. 'I may be an insensitive clod, but I'm not blind. That week I stayed in your house, even I saw that you positively glowed.'

Nicole slid over to his side so that they were barely touching, then put a hand on his arm and looked earnestly up into his face. 'But don't you see? That's because you were there. I was every bit as happy that week in San Francisco at your place, and there wasn't an elegant social affair in sight.'

Dirk stared intently at her, the green eyes burning into hers. 'Lord, Nicole,' he said at last in a harsh, rasping voice, 'if I thought there was a chance for us——' He broke off and swept a hand over his tousled dark hair. 'I can't tell you what hell it's been without you, believing I'd never see you again. You brought a light into my life that I thought had gone out for good when you left me.'

The sun had set by now, and the lengthening shadows darkened the room. Still, she could just make out his strong features, the light of love in his eyes, the slow bright gleam of desire.

She reached out and put a hand on his face. 'I'll never leave you again, Dirk,' she said slowly. 'I love you. I want to be with you, forever. We can work it out. As you said that night, other couples do.'

He took her hand away from his cheek and pressed it to his lips. Then he gave a low groan, his arms came around her and he buried his dark head in the crook of her neck. Nicole stroked his hair back from his forehead, holding him close, and they clung to each other tightly, wordlessly, for several long, wonderful moments.

Then he raised his head to gaze down into her eyes. 'I'll radio for the helicopter tomorrow. We can get married in Cutbank.' She nodded happily, speechless with joy. 'And,' he went on, 'I've been thinking. The job they offered me at UCLA was very tempting. We could spend part of the year down there, close to your father and friends. You wouldn't even have to come on expeditions with me if you didn't want to.'

'Whatever you say, darling,' she murmured. 'But I want to go wherever you go.' She smiled up at him. 'Now that you've trained me so well, I've become indispensable to you.'

'In more ways than you'll ever know,' he said.

He pulled her up against him, and his mouth came down on hers in a passionate, demanding, penetrating kiss. Slowly his weight propelled her backwards on the couch until he was lying half on top of her, and his hand slid down to cover her breast.

With fumbling, impatient fingers, he began to unbutton the red shirt, and when she felt his warm hands on her bare skin she leaned her head back with a sigh, certain now she'd done the right thing.

She felt as though she was home at last, where she truly belonged. Two different worlds could meet and become one, she thought dreamily, with love to guide the way.

HARLEQUIN
Romance

A Christmas tradition...

Imagine spending Christmas in New
Orleans with a blind stranger and his aged
guide dog—when you're supposed to be
there on your honeymoon!
#3163 Every Kind of Heaven
by Bethany Campbell

Imagine spending Christmas with a man
you once "married"—in a mock ceremony
at the age of eight!
#3166 The Forgetful Bride
by Debbie Macomber

*Available in December 1991, wherever
Harlequin books are sold.*

Take 4 bestselling love stories FREE
Plus get a FREE surprise gift!

HARLEQUIN
PROUDLY PRESENTS
A DAZZLING NEW CONCEPT IN ROMANCE FICTION

One small town—twelve terrific love stories

Welcome to Tyler, Wisconsin—a town full of people
you'll enjoy getting to know, memorable friends and
unforgettable lovers, and a long-buried secret that
lurks beneath its serene surface....

JOIN US FOR A YEAR IN THE LIFE OF TYLER

Each book set in Tyler is a self-contained love story;
together, the twelve novels stitch the fabric of a
community.

LOSE YOUR HEART TO TYLER!

The excitement begins in March 1992, with
WHIRLWIND, by Nancy Martin. When lively, brash
Liza Baron arrives home unexpectedly, she moves
into the old family lodge, where the silent and
mysterious Cliff Forrester has been living in seclusion
for years....

WATCH FOR ALL TWELVE BOOKS
OF THE TYLER SERIES
Available wherever Harlequin books are sold

TYLER-G